Sabine Baring-Gould

Court Royal

A Story of cross Currents - Vol. I

Sabine Baring-Gould

Court Royal
A Story of cross Currents - Vol. I

ISBN/EAN: 9783337082611

Printed in Europe, USA, Canada, Australia, Japan

Cover: Foto ©Andreas Hilbeck / pixelio.de

More available books at **www.hansebooks.com**

COURT ROYAL

A STORY OF CROSS CURRENTS

BY THE

AUTHOR OF 'MEHALAH' 'JOHN HERRING' &c.

IN THREE VOLUMES

VOL. I.

LONDON

SMITH, ELDER, & CO., 15 WATERLOO PLACE

1886

PREFACE.

When in 1880 the author published 'Mehalah,' his critics, public and private, attacked him or remonstrated with him because there was no moral to the story—because 'Mehalah' was not, as the Germans would say, a *Tendenz-roman*. No doubt that life is but an acted Æsop's Fables, in which the actors are human, but it is surely allowable in an author to take wings occasionally, and fly away from the stings and goads of moral applications which prog one in everyday life, into the region of unmoralising fancy. However, in his second attempt, 'John Herring,' he did have a moral purpose throughout his story, and his critics, public and private, with one accord—only excepting a couple of Scottish reviewers—failed to see it. He complained of this one day to one of his critics, who replied, 'We have no time to dive for purposes, we skim for story.' That is true generally of the English reader, specially of the novel reader, who dips but does not plunge. Therefore the author acknowledges that he made a mistake. A purpose, a moral, must not be sunk in the depths like a pearl, but tossed up on the margin as the amber, conspicuous to the first passer-by.

His object in 'John Herring' was to show that man's character is only moulded by mistakes. His reviewers objected that his hero was characterless : that was his purpose—to show an amiable, well-intentioned man, shaped by his misfortunes. There was another, and deeper, purpose in the story, which was to show how a noble character can only be formed which has before it an ideal, and that the ideal which elevates character is ever, and ever must be, unattainable. The man without an ideal sinks; the man with one rises; but in so rising passes through agonies. *This* life is his purgatory. Only the man without an ideal is happy—brutally happy.

And now the author will correct his previous error, and expose the purpose of this new story at the outset. To do this, he will tell the story of its inception.

In the summer of 1883, as he was returning from his holiday in Tyrol, he came across an account of a Croatian mother who, in a state of absolute destitution, pawned her child to save its life and prolong her own. He occupied and amused himself, during his railway journey home, in trying to work out what would be the moral and mental result in such an instance, supposing the child to be a girl endowed by nature with generous emotions and considerable shrewdness. It struck him that such a character, so developed, would be typical of the individualism and impatience of restraint, social, moral, and religious, combined with impulsive generosity, which is the feature of the new civilisation, about also to be the motive force of the future, that is coming everywhere to the front.

He had read recently a Polish story, entitled 'Morituri,' which depicted the decay of a Polish princely race, and it occurred to the author to take such a family, steeped in traditional culture, infused with feudal-Christian morality, as the representative of the old civilisation which is melting and disappearing everywhere, as the other becomes concrete and asserts itself.

Again, the author asked himself, What would be the result, what the mutual action and reaction, if such a line of life as that which he had ideally traced in one of his heroines—the representative of the Coming Age—were run athwart the threads of old culture and ethics? Would each act on the other at all, to modify its peculiarities and broaden its view of life? To take another simile, would such a vein of molten, fiery, nineteenth-century individuality, operating vertically, do other than shatter the superincumbent, horizontal social beds? Would it be itself at all metamorphosed in the process?

The author was teased by the problem that rose continually in his brain. He felt that he could only work it out by calling his representative characters out of the vasty deep of conjecture, and setting them on the table, giving them souls, and letting them move and act towards each other automatically, and work out the problem for themselves. Such, then, is the history of the genesis of this story, and the reader is requested to bear its purpose in mind as he skims it. Two types in two groups are opposed to each other; each group represents a set of ideas, social and moral, the one coming on, conquering, overwhelming, the other disappearing and likely soon to be looked back upon as having become extinct in the moral world like asceticism and mysticism. There are two heroines each the focusing of the good qualities of the two groups, and two heroes each the concentration of the infirmities of the same.

CONTENTS

OF

THE FIRST VOLUME.

—◆◇◆—

COURT ROYAL.

A STORY OF CROSS CURRENTS.

————◆◆————

CHAPTER I.

A LITTLE DEVIL.

AT the top or at the bottom? At which shall we begin? Sediment to-day is scum to-morrow. That which is on the surface sinks. Therefore, does it matter? The universe is in revolution, so is the social order. We will begin at the bottom, as most philosophical. Only the builders of Lagado began their edifices at the apex. The Barbican is the oldest portion of ancient Plymouth. It consists of a collection of crazy houses built along the quay of Sutton Pool, which was the ancient port of Plymouth. The houses are tall, with slated fronts and bow windows, much out of the perpendicular, of various dates. In these houses

VOL. I.

dwelt the old merchants of Plymouth, who equipped vessels against the Spaniards and carried Tavistock friezes to all the ports of Europe. From Sutton Pool Drake sailed against the Armada. The grand merchant-houses have become the habitations of dealers in marine stores, drinking-shops and eating-houses.

Sic transit gloria mundi.

The houses on the Barbican are so crowded that they are devoid of back yards, and when the inhabitants have a washing they thrust their garments from their windows on poles to dry in the sea-breeze and the sun. Some ingenious dwellers in these old houses contrive a system of rigging between their poles whereby a much larger wash can be exposed. On every day that lends itself to drying, the Barbican flutters its flags and streamers. The flags vary in shape, more than in colour, and most of all in their heraldic achievements. Some are 'enhanced' with flaunches, others with bendlets, frets, bordures, even with bars sinister. Certain bifurcated pennons show a leaning towards 'escutcheoning.' The banners are for the most part white, tawny as old Tiber, or Isabelle. Some few are azure of a deep and dingy blue.

From one window a circular mass of drapery, gules, bulges in the wind. It is the petticoat of the lady of the ham and sausage shop.

One corner house, standing between two thoroughfares, never displayed its bunting. Apparently, no washing was ever done in it. Over the door of this house hung three golden balls, and in scaling paint over the window was inscribed the name—'LAZARUS.'

The Barbican is not a savoury place. Here the fish are unladen and sold, and here the little fish that fall out of the baskets get trampled out of shape, and rot in the mire.

When the tide is out, the ooze in Sutton Pool sends up its complement of effluvium. Providentially, the sea-tangles, hanging from the wharf in fringes of dull green, exhale chlorine, and the sea-breeze brings in ozone, to disinfect and disperse the pestilential odours.

The Barbican is a busy place all day, and late into the night; but at noon, for an hour, it drops into quiet. Then all the sound that habitually pervades it is sucked in at the doors of the taverns and eating-houses, and fills them to repletion.

It was precisely at this hour, one hot day in early June, that the stillness of the Barbican quay was broken by piercing and protracted shrieks.

Two persons and a cat alone occupied the wharf at that time : the one was the pier-guard, who was then lounging on the wall looking seaward ; the other was an old woman sitting under a large umbrella with her back to sun and sea, fast asleep before the table of gingerbeer-bottles of which she disposed. The cat took no notice of the screams, nor did the old woman, who only woke when the quay became repeopled and business looked alive. The guard turned leisurely round, drew his hands out of his pockets, walked to the steps by which passengers disembarked from the Oreston steamer, descended them, cast off a boat, and, stepping in, shouted, 'Hold hard, you little devil!'

Some faces, attracted by the cries, appeared at the windows, but the view was obscured by fluttering drapery. The lady over the ham and sausage shop, Thresher by name, saw what was the matter; her visual ray was not cut off by the washing. She shouted some practical advice, then turned and scolded her husband, who lay on the bed with his boots upon the pillow, reading a Radical paper. After that she drew on a jacket and descended to the quay.

Some men, moreover, who had finished their dinner, issued from the eating-houses to ascertain what was the matter, and those who had not done bolted the rest of their food, fearful of being too late for an accident, yet unwilling to leave unconsumed good victuals for which they had paid.

The screams became louder, shriller. Then they were interrupted for a minute, again to ring forth as loudly as before.

The cries issued from the lungs of a child— a girl—of twelve, who was in the arms of a wretched-looking woman. They were near the edge of the quay when the screams began. The woman was attempting to fling herself and the child into the water. The girl had her arms about an old cannon, planted in the granite coping as a hold for hawsers, and clung to it desperately. Finally, the superior strength of the woman prevailed, and she precipitated herself and the child over the edge into the Pool. Then, for a moment, the cries were silenced, for a moment only, while the child was under water. Both rose to the surface, covered with mud, near a chain. In a moment, the child saw her opportunity, grasped the chain, and crawled up it, with the water streaming from her, looking like a drowning rat, and again she shrieked as loud as her lungs would allow.

In a moment, also, the pierkeeper was at hand in the boat. He lifted the woman out of the water, and then laid hold of the child. The latter, unable at first to distinguish that the hands grasping her were not those of her mother, and that the object for which she was grasped was not to drown her, clung frantically to the chain, and yelled with such force and penetration in the tones, that the guard lost patience, and said angrily, 'Let go, you squalling cat, will you?'

Instantly the child relaxed her hold, and allowed herself to be lifted into the boat. She knew, by the voice, that she was in the hands of a man, come to save her. When she was in the boat, she dipped her palms in the water, and washed the mud from her eyes and mouth and nose. After that she set herself to clean the face of her mother with the skirt of her frock.

'What is the meaning of this?' said the man.

'I wouldn't be drownded,' answered the child. 'I told mother as much, but her paid no heed to what I said.'

'Now then, missus,' said he, addressing the woman with rough kindness, 'what did you do it for?'

The poor creature made no reply. She sat, cuddled into a heap in the bottom, hugging her knees, with the water pouring off her. Her head was bowed on her bosom.

'Did y' hear, now?' shouted the child, raising the sodden hair off the mother's ear. 'The gemman asked you a civil question, and you must answer him civil too. He asked you what made you do it.'

'I am wretched,' she replied in a faint voice; 'my husband is dead. We have been starving. I can find no situation because of Joanna, and get no work. I did not know what to do with myself and her, and as us couldn't find a situation on earth, I thought we'd go and get one in heaven.'

'But I wouldn't,' put in the girl, emphatically, looking the boatman level in the eyes. 'I told mother plain I was not agreeable. I don't want to go to heaven—and,' with a stamp on the bottom of the boat, 'I won't go.'

'You've a will of your own, apparently,' said the man, smiling.

'I don't choose to be drownded,' answered the girl. Then she thrust her wet and dirty hair out of her face, and tried to knot it behind her

head, ' and I don't choose as mother shall be,
neither.'

'I'll tell you what, ma'am,' said the pierkeeper ; 'two good things have combined for
the saving of you to-day. First comes I. I
was on the spot handy. Secondly, the tide was
running out and leaving the Pool dry ; so there
was no depth available for drowning purposes.'
The boat touched the steps. 'Up with you,
both,' he said, 'and mind, no more of these
games.'

The wretched woman obeyed meekly. The
child strode up the stone stairs full of confidence,
saying, but hardly in a tone of apology, ' You
know, mother, I was not agreeable.'

The woman staggered after her daughter
to the pier, and then stood there helpless,
dazed, looking about her without light in her
eyes.

The water ran off her and formed a pond at
her feet ; the slime was smeared over her hair
and face and hands. Her soaked garments
clung to her, revealing at once how few and thin
they were.

By this time several persons had assembled.
They surrounded the little group and eyed them
curiously. These were mostly men, still chew-

ing the remains of their dinner or picking their teeth. Mrs. Thresher, from the ham-shop, was there in a black body over a red petticoat, very short, exposing dirty stockings and slippers down at heel.

Questions showered on the poor creature, which she did not answer, perhaps did not catch. She clutched her child's hand convulsively, and with disengaged hand wiped the water from her eyes.

'Now look you here,' said the pier-guard, ' you oughtn't to have done it, or if you did ought to do it, you ought to have done it in a less dirty place. Sutton Pool is not a palatable place in which to end existence. Wait till the tide is out, and have a look for yourself. I reckon further acquaintance won't make you more friendly. It will rince all taste of felo-de-se out of your mouth. Dead cats, rotten cabbage, decayed potatoes, cracked cloam (crockery), old tobacco pipes, kettles and pans full of holes, boots bursted, and soleless shoes, scatted (broken) bottles, anything, everything that goes to make filth is chucked in there, and rots away into black paste which is proper consolidated smeech (smell). I reckon that Sutton Pool bottom is made of the dirtiest dregs of

civilisation. That is what we've hauled you
and your brat out of. If you've any sense of
decency in you, keep out of Sutton Pool. The
blue sea is a different crib altogether.'

'I won't be drownded neither in the blue
sea, nor in Sutton Pool, nor in a pickling-tub,'
said the child resolutely; 'I'm damned if I
be.'

The circle of lookers-on burst out laughing.

'Oh, you wicked child!' exclaimed Mrs.
Thresher, of the ham-shop. 'Where do you
expect to go, using them swearing words?'

'Father said it when he meant a thing—
much,' answered the child.

'Your father smoked, I reckon.'

'Yes, he did.'

'But you don't see ladies smoke.'

'No.'

'Well,' said Mrs. Thresher, 'pipes and
cusses are nat'ral in a man's mouth, but natur'
herself protests when you see either in the mouth
of a woman.'

'Did you hear how the little creature
squealed?' asked the pierkeeper.

'Her cries drew me from my dinner, and
lost me the picking of my rabbit-bones,' said one
of the men.

'I'd have had another glass of ale,' said a second, 'but I thought two foreigners was fighting and sticking knives into each other. I wouldn't ha' missed *that*. I was always a bit of a sportsman since I was a boy.'

'I cried,' said the girl, 'because I would not let mother drown me.'

'And cry tha' did, by jiggers!' exclaimed a skipper, a large man from Yorkshire. 'I was down in my cabin when tha' piped.'

'Look here,' said the pier-guard; 'if us stand here in a knot, the police will be suspecting something and turn their beaks this way. Then they'll have this unfortunate female up before the magistrates on the double charge of felo-de-se and felo-de-child, and transport her for it to Dartmoor. So let us be moving. Now then, ma'am!'—he spoke to the woman, planting himself before her, legs apart, and his hands on his hips—'if you will pass your word that you won't play no more of these pranks, I'll let you go; if not, I'll tow you into custody myself.'

'No, sir, I won't do it no more,' said the miserable creature.

'Her sha'n't!' protested the child.

'What is to be done with them?' asked

the pierman. 'They are both wet to the marrow
of their bones.'

No one was prepared with an answer.
One man, suspecting a subscription, tailed
away.

'You must go home and have a change,'
said the pierman kindly. 'And let me counsel
a drop of hot grog. It will drive the chill out
of you and the squealer.'

'I have no home—I have no change!
I have nowhere and nothing,' answered the
woman mournfully.

'There is that blessed institootion, the
Work'us, always open,' said one man in a tone
of sarcasm.

'I'd rather drown than go there,' answered
she; 'there they'd take my Joanna from me.'

A grunt of assent.

'Her's got the proper principles of a Christian,' said the woman in the red petticoat. 'I'd
go into Sutton Pool myself rather than into the
House. I reckon in the matter of dirt they're
about equal, only in the House it's moral, and in
the Pool its physical.'

'Sither, lass,' said the skipper, in strong
Yorkshire accent, 'how didst 'a come here?
Tell us all aboot it.'

'My husband died,' she answered timidly;
'I sold everything I had, bit by bit, till all was
gone. I couldn't pay my rent, and I couldn't
buy no food. I went from place to place after
work, but I could get none. No one would
give me a situation till I got rid of the child.
All were in one song—"Send her to the Union."
I couldn't do that; so I thought we'd both go
to heaven together.'

'Have you no change of clothes anywhere?'
asked Mrs. Thresher; 'because, if you have,
you may change in my room, and I'll turn my
old man out while you do it.'

'I've naught but what I stand up in,' said
the poor creature, 'nor has Joanna, neither.'

'Now, then, my lads,' said the pierman,
casting his eye round, 'I propose we raise a
few shillings among us to rig out the pair afresh.'

'I reckon Mr. Lazarus can fit them out,'
said one of the bystanders.

'O' course he can,' said the skipper; 'but
he'll not do 't wi'out brass. Here's half a crown
to start wi'. Who'll give something upon that?
Here's my cap as collecting-box.'

'It 'll come expensive,' remarked a barge-
man in sepulchral tones; 'I know what the
rig-out of my missus costs me.'

'A gown can be had secondhand for a trifle.'

'A gown ain't all,' said the bargeman mysteriously.

'What else, then?'

'What else? Why, there's stays,' growled the bargeman. 'Them figures—new—seven and eightpence three-farthings!'

'Then there's a petticoat,' suggested a pilot timidly; 'if you doubt my word look around at all the fluttering bunting. Women must wear them things somehow, and they don't use 'em as caps.'

'*A* petticoat!' exclaimed the north-country skipper. 'Every respectable lass has two—one coloured, t'other white.'

'Must the little maid have stays, too!' asked the pierkeeper.

'All females has stays,' answered the barge-man. 'Girls has 'em without bones. The bones come later in life.'

'What more?' asked the skipper.

A dead silence. The men were thinking and looking inquiringly at the dripping woman, who was too bewildered to reply.

'Where is Mrs. Thresher? her can tell us,' said the pilot.

But Mrs. Thresher was gone to her room to turn her old man out of it, and prepare for the contingency of receiving the poor woman into it.

Still silence. The men's brows were wrinkled with hard thought. It was broken by the rumbling bass of the bargeman. 'Dress-improver!'

'Must the little maid have one?'

'Of course. All females have dress-improvers,' said the bargeman, puffing and swelling with consciousness of superior knowledge. 'Four-and-ten is about the figure.'

'That makes five articles apiece, mates,' said the pierkeeper, checking them off on his fingers: 'thumb for gown, fore and middle fingers stand for petticoats, the last but one for stays, and the little chap is dress-improver. Now, then, mates, see what we can raise among us for the poor creatures.'

The party moved along the quay towards the pawnshop, the Yorkshire skipper revolving, cap in hand, among the members.

'I've been considering,' said he, after a while, 'as how I might find the lass a berth aboard my vessel if she could get shut (rid) of the bairn. We could do wi' a woman to cook and wash for us; and shoo might addle (earn) a few shillings that road. What do you think o' that, mates? And what dost 'a say to it thysel', lass?'

The dazed woman looked at the Yorkshire-man without understanding his proposal. He repeated it in more intelligible form; then she comprehended it, and her wan face lighted up, only to dull again.

'May I take my Joanna?'

'That's the scratch,' said the skipper. 'Shoo's wick as a scoprill (lively as a teetotum), and I'd be glad if I could; but we can't find room for little bairns.'

The pilot explained: 'Can't find room on board for little maidens.'

'What is to become of my Joanna?' asked the bewildered woman, looking with blank eyes about her.

The man with a vein of sarcasm in him, who had before suggested the Union, threw out another suggestion, likewise ironical. 'As you're about to get clothes of Mr. Lazarus, perhaps you can pawn the child to him, and raise a few shillings on her!'

The suggestion elicited a general laugh. The woman, however, took it seriously, and walked towards the pawnbroker's shop, drawing the child along with her.

'Here is t'brass a've gotten together for thee,' said the skipper, pouring the coin from his cap into her hand. 'Take it, and get the ten articles thyself.'

Then he signed to the others to withdraw, and they, with great delicacy, did so, whilst the woman entered the pawnbroker's shop.

'Mates,' said the skipper, 'leave the lass to do the shopping alone. It's more decent. She'll get the ten articles. Trust a woman to bargain. And whilst shoo's aboot it we'll put heads together and consider what is to be done wi' the little bairn.'

'Did you hear her scream?' asked the pilot.

'Her 'd do as a syren (steam whistle) to an ironclad, and rouse the Three Towns (Plymouth, Stonehouse, and Devonport) when coming into harbour.'

'Scream!' exclaimed another man, 'I should like to know what man or woman but the old lady under the umbrella by the ginger-beer could fail to hear her. Mark my words! That little maid ain't born to be drowned. How her worked her way up the chain out o' the slime! Well,' sententiously, 'there be other chains than that in this world; and may she work herself up the next she catches as well as she went up that!'

CHAPTER II.

PAWNED.

THE woman entered the shop of Mr. Lazarus. When there she stood trembling and looking down, confused or frightened, whilst the child at her side peered about with eager eyes at the articles with which the shop was crowded.

Mr. Lazarus was a dark man, of distinct Israelitish type, his hair cut short, like moleskin, but his jaws and chin covered with a bristly scrub. He was wont to shave once a week, and went bristly and black between times. His eye ran over the customer, and took stock of what she wore. He soon satisfied himself that she had nothing about her in his way, except a gold wedding-ring.

Mr. Lazarus looked suspiciously and threateningly at the child. He detested children. They played marbles, ball, tipcat on the pavement, and broke his windows. They shouted

after him, 'Rags and bones!' or 'Old clo'!'
through their noses, or put their heads into his
shop, and asked how he was off for soap, or
'Any black puddings or bacon rashers to-
day.'

The pawnbroker was frequently engaged,
behind his counter, whittling at a stick, lying
in wait to rush forth with it upon the urchins
who offended him. It was rarely, however,
that he caught the delinquents. He more often
fell upon, or fell over, an inoffensive and unof-
fending child, and rattled his stick about its
sides. Then the parents—the mother certainly
—would appear on the scene and join in the
noise, belabouring Mr. Lazarus with her tongue.
When matters reached this point, Mr. Lazarus
would return to his shop, with the stick tucked
under his arm, growling Levitical imprecations.

'What do you want?' asked Mr. Lazarus,
looking up from an account-book, and laying
the stick on the table.

'Please, sir,' answered the woman in a faint,
frightened voice, 'I want a set of dry clothes
for myself and Joanna.'

'Certainly,' answered the Jew with alacrity.
'Tumbled into the Pool, eh? About what
figure, pray?'

'This is all I have,' answered she, extending her hand and opening it.

'One half-crown, two shillings, one'—he rang it—'bad, two sixpences, and eight threepenny bits, also one French ha'penny, which don't pass current. I return you the shilling. You may be able to get others to take it, less wide-awake. That makes six-and-six. Can't do much for you at that price.'

Then the poor creature said, 'Please, sir, you'll be liberal, I hope. I've nothing else, and am wet to the marrow. I have brought the child. I thought to raise a few shillings on her.'

'The child! What do you mean?'

'My darling, my Joanna.'

Mr. Lazarus turned a green hue.

'You're trying to make sport of me!' he exclaimed, clutching at his stick. 'You've been put up to it. I won't stand this sort of game. Get out at once.'

'Please, sir,' said the woman, trembling with cold and alarm, 'the gentleman outside as fished me from the Pool got up a subscription for me, that I might have dry clothes. I've no more, but if you'd consent to take the child——'

'I take the child—I—I!' screamed Mr.

Lazarus. ' Children are the plague of my life. I wouldn't have one if offered for nothing.'

' Then, sir, I must take the money elsewhere.'

' Oh !' said the pawnbroker, ' six-and-six is it? Pity it should be lost. Do you think the gentlemen would subscribe a little more? The charitable feelings, when well worked, are very yielding. If you'd make believe to be desperate, and about to fall or throw yourself in again, may be the collecting cap would go round again, and the sum disposable mount to eleven-and-six. At eleven-and-six I might consider you. I can't so much as look at you for six-and-six. Just cast your eyes over this myrtle-green trimmed with cream lace ! Don't it make your mouth water? '

' I'm watering all over,' sighed the woman. ' I only want ordinary dry clothes.'

' Or this Dolly Varden with panniers, a little passed in style, and a kiss-me-quick bonnet. Make you quite irresistible, miss— beg pardon—ma'am, I mean.'

' I have no more. I can get no more. I need only a cotton dress and underclothing.'

' Lor' bless you !' exclaimed the Jew, ' what does that latter signify so long as the gown is gorgeous? Try to screw some more from the gents outside. If you cried, now, in a proper heart-rending way?'

The woman shook her head despairingly. 'I did not ask for this. I want only necessaries. Why did they not let me drown, and be at rest?'

'What, ma'am?' said the Jew. 'Drown with an available six-and-six on the quay awaiting you! The thing is ridiculous!'

'Please, sir, will you take the child?'

'What do you mean?' asked Lazarus testily, turning green again.

'I mean my Joanna,' answered the woman, pointing to the little girl at her side.

Mr. Lazarus waxed wroth. 'Do I take little girls? Eh! look round and see what are the articles in my shop. Dolls; yes, they don't eat. China figures; yes, they don't wear out clothes. I'm not a cannibal. Can't make butcher's meat out of children. I wish I might. I'd set up shambles and reduce their numbers.'

'I don't want to sell Joanna,' said the woman in a dull, distressed voice, 'I wouldn't sell her for a thousand guineas. But I thought, no offence, I might pawn her for a time, so as to make up the difference, and get a fit out of dry clothes for both of us.'

'Be off with you! This is no foundling hospital where every troublesome child may be left. Get out of this, or I'll rattle my stick about the bones of the monkey.'

'I have nowhere to go to, sir. I have passed my word not to fling myself into the sea again. You shall have Joanna, sir, for half-a-sovereign.'

'Half-a-sovereign!' cried Mr. Lazarus, starting back. 'Have I human ears to hear such a proposition? Half-a-sovereign for a little maggot that'll eat her own weight of nourishing victuals every day! I won't have her at any price. Chuck her into Sutton Pool.'

'I won't be drownded,' said the child resolutely.

'I throwed her in once, and her crawled out like a spider running along its cobweb.'

'Do with her what you will. I'll have nothing to say to her,' cried the angry pawn-broker. Then working himself into fury, 'Will you be off? Look what a pond you two have made in my shop. The floor is swimming. A mop won't take it up in a week ; and all the iron-ware, and the forks and knives, will be rusted, and the cloth and leather mildewed.'

'Well, sir,' sighed the woman, 'give me back the money and I'll go.'

'Six-and-six!' said Mr. Lazarus in a softer tone, 'six-and-six *is* six-and-six. Can't we deal reasonably and quietly? What is the advantage of your working yourself up into fever and fury?'

'Please, sir,' said the woman with pertinacity, such as could hardly be looked for in one so timid and dazed, 'I can have a situation if I get rid of the child.'

'Well, what is that to me?'

'I won't sell her, sir! and I won't send her to the Union. If you'll be so kind as to take her, and lend me half-a-sovereign on her, I'll throw in my wedding-ring beside.'

'Let me look at it. I dare be sworn it is brass.'

'We were well off when us married, and could afford it,' explained the woman. Then, whilst the Jew was examining the ring and testing it with acid, she said, 'My Joanna is of pure gold. You'd better take her, sir. You'd never repent. I reckon she can do most things. Her can wash——'

'I have no washing done here,' said Lazarus, shortly. 'Never found the need. The Barbican is poisoned with the smell of yellow soap and the reek of drying linen.'

'Then, sir, her can cook you a rasher of bacon——'

'I never eat of the pig,' screamed Lazarus, and spat on the floor.

'Her can kindle a fire——'

'And waste tons of coal.'

'Her can nurse the babies——'

'I've no babies. I don't want 'em. I wouldn't have 'em.'

'Her can run messages like a greyhound, and mind the shop when you are out ; and should burglars try to break in, her would scream, and scream, and scream.'

'Eh !' said Lazarus, looking up interested. 'Was that she screaming half-an-hour ago ?'

'It was. Her can scream when proper. Other times she's as still as a mouse.'

Mr. Lazarus considered for a few moments. He rubbed his bristly chin, blew his nose in a fashion almost lost in this age of refinement. Then he leaned both elbows on the counter and stared at the girl. Mr. Lazarus was nervous about burglars. Unwittingly the mother had touched a fibre in his soul that quivered. Report credited him with vast wealth, with money, plate, jewellery, stored in the crazy old house. More than once he had been alarmed by attempts to break in. He had an infirmity which he could not master. He slept so soundly that nothing woke him. The Barbican was a noisy place by night as well as by day. Tipsy sailors rambled about it, drunken women squabbled, foreign sailors fought on the quay. The ear in time became so accustomed to noises that they ceased to disturb. Lazarus had resolved to get a dog, but begrudged the food it would consume. Following this train of thought, he said to himself, 'Half-a-sov. ! I could get a mongrel pup for less.'

'Sir,' argued the woman, 'with a pup you wouldn't get a gold wedding-ring.'

'That is true, but a dog eats bones, and girls eat meat.'

'Oh! my Joanna hasn't much of that. A crust of bread and some dripping—her never gets beyond that. Besides, you'd have to pay tax on a dog, not on a girl.'

'That also is true, but a dog grows his own coat, and a girl grows out of every suit you put her into.'

'The girl is a golden girl, gold through and through,' said the mother. 'She wakes early, and has her hand in work all day ; is never idle, never plays, never neglects a duty ; try her.'

Mr. Lazarus came from behind the counter, put his hand under Joanna's chin and thrust the wet hair from her brow. He pursed up his lips, half closed his eyes, and studied her critically.

Then Joanna, surmising that Mr. Lazarus was about to relent, put forth her full powers of resistance. She clawed at his coat, which being rusty gave way ; she bit at his hands, and made them bleed ; she kicked his shins, and forced him to caper ; and she yelled, as surely no mortal lungs had yelled before.

The men outside drew near the shop, flattened their noses against the window-panes and looked in, then grinned, rubbed their hands, laughed in each other's faces, and said : 'Her's born to make a noise in the world, no mistake—an irrepressible. Then they backed. The screams pierced the drums of their ears like bradawls.

Joanna danced and tore, and shrieked and writhed. 'I am not good,' she cried ; 'I am not golden. I am bad, and brazen. I'm a little devil. Don't buy me. I'm worth nothing

at all. I scream all day. All night as well.
No one can sleep in the house where I am. I
never work. I scat (break) all the cloam
(crockery). I smash the windows. I set a
house on fire. I'm a devil; I'm a devil.'

In vain did the poor mother reason with,
and try to pacify the child. The little creature
was as one possessed. She shook herself in
convulsions of rage, so that the water spirted
off her, as from a poodle drying itself after a
bath.

Mr. Lazarus was fain to put the counter
between himself and the child. He was not
angry; he looked on approvingly.

'With burglars,' said he, nodding to the
mother, ' this would be first-rate.'

Then the girl tore round the shop, kicking
the counter, and dashing against the goods piled
in the corners.

'Look here!' said Mr. Lazarus. 'Do you
see all these walking-sticks? Thorn and bamboo
they are. I'll try their respective merits on
your ribs, you wild cat, unless you desist.'
Then to the mother, ' She will do. I take her.
You shall have the money. I must stop the
noise first; there is no dealing because of it.'

Then, feebly assisted by the woman, the

pawnbroker carried the child, kicking, tearing, howling, into the kitchen, to the coalhole, into which he thrust her. Then he tried to lock her in, but she dashed herself against the door, and beat the lock when he attempted to fasten it. After many efforts he succeeded in turning the key.

'There,' said he, 'squall yourself hoarse. Bang your hands and knees raw. No one will heed.'

He returned to the shop with the mother, who was trembling and crying.

He shut the kitchen door, and the shop door leading into the house likewise; nevertheless the cries and thumpings from the coalhole were still audible, though distant and muffled.

Mr. Lazarus wiped his brow. 'There is life in the child. There are will and pertinacity,' he said. 'She knows her own mind, which is more than do many. Here is the half-sovereign.'

'Thank you, sir. You understand, I don't sell her.'

'Of course not, of course not.'

'I only pawn her,' said the woman timidly.

'To be sure, to be sure.'

'And, sir, I want my ticket.'

' What ticket? '

' The pawn-ticket, sir, so that when I bring the money I may have my child back out of pawn.'

' By all means,' said Mr. Lazurus. ' And when shall we say the time is up? '

' Well, sir, if I may make it seven years, I'll take it as a favour. Joanna is now twelve, and in seven she'll be nineteen. I may be able to redeem her in a few months, but I cannot tell. I'm going away in a ship, and I don't know where to. I should like a margin, so as to give me plenty of time to look about, and scrape.'

' Certainly,' said Mr. Lazarus. ' Seven years let it be. The interest will be ten per cent. A shilling a year. In seven years that will be seven shillings for interest. I'll write you out the ticket at once. Hand me over the wedding-ring again. You took it up just now. The half-sovereign and six-and-six—less twopence for the ticket, that makes sixteen-and-four. This is what you want to lay out in dry clothes. We will see if we can suit you. The myrtle-green and cream lace won't do. Style unbecoming. Something warm and useful. I understand. Here is the ticket. Number six

hundred and seventeen your daughter is,
ma'am. Six hundred and seventeen. Now
your name, please?'

'Marianne Rosevere.'

'And my little maid is——'

'Six hundred and seventeen.'

CHAPTER III.

LAZARUS.

WHEN the mother was gone, with dry and decent garments, and the drumming and roaring at the cellar door had ceased, Mr. Lazarus went to the coalhole and unlocked it.

Then Joanna walked forth. She had gone in wet; she emerged caked in coal-dust, black as a sweep. Clothing, hands, face, hair, were all black. Nothing was clean about her but the white of her eyes, her red lips and shining teeth.

Mr. Lazarus held the door and stood back. He expected her to fly forth, snapping and snarling like a spiteful dog. He feared for his shins, and therefore held a stick for protection. But Joanna came forth composedly, without a word.

'I must confess,' said the pawnbroker, reassured, 'you *do* look like a little devil.' I

don't think you could come it more natural,
got up for the occasion with theatrical pro-
perties.'

'I am not a little devil,' said the girl, standing in the midst of the kitchen, and looking at
Mr. Lazarus. 'I am a girl; I am not bad, I
am good; I am gold, not brass; I am not idle,
I work hard; I rise early; I break nothing; I
knit; I sew; I cook; I scream. Where is
my mother? Is she gone?'

'Gone, gone right away on end. She has
pawned you to me for seven years; raised ten
shillings on you—more than you are worth, if
coined.'

'I am worth more than ten shillings; I
am worth ten pounds.'

'You understand you can't go to mother;
you are pawned. If your mother does not
come back in seven years, then you fall to me
altogether as my own. Do you understand?'

'Yes,' said the girl. 'Mother has pawned
everything else she had down to me. Now is
my turn. I will stay.'

'Your number is six hundred and seventeen.
Look in my ledger; there you are till cancelled.
Why did you scream so horribly?'

'Because I wanted to be with mother.'

'And now you are content to remain with me?'

'I am pawned; I can't help myself. Mother has raised the money on me. I must stay till she returns with the ticket and the half-sovereign.'

'And the interest—the interest at ten per cent.,' insisted Mr. Lazarus.

'I know nothing about that,' said the girl. 'I will stay till mother brings the money. I cannot help myself.'

'Come along, you squalling cockatoo,' said the pawnbroker; 'I will show you over the place, and tell you what your work will be. This is the kitchen.'

'And that is your nose. I have eyes. You wouldn't make me believe this a parlour if you swore to it.'

'You are a queer imp.'

'I am good,' said the girl. 'I will cook the dinner, and then you will say the same.'

'No waste of coals here,' observed Lazarus gravely. 'To think of the profligate waste among the rich! The tons of coal they burn; nothing to show for it but smoke and ashes! I never turned a penny by coals in all my life, never.'

'I have,' said Joanna.

'I shall be glad to hear how you managed that.'

'It was this way. We'd a little garden ran down to the water, where the coal-barges went by. I corked an empty soda-water bottle and hung it to the branch of an apple-tree. When the bargemen went by they couldn't hold off having a shy at the bottle, and they shied lumps of coal. I went out every day with a shovel. We kept the kitchen fire with that bottle, and the beauty was she never broke. Couldn't, you understand, because her swung when hit.'

Lazarus looked at the child with admiration. 'Beautiful! upon my word, beautiful! You are a genius, Six hundred and seventeen. Follow me.'

He led her into the shop. 'There,' he said, 'you sleep under the counter. There are blankets about to make a bed of. Only mind everything goes back into place in the morning; nothing torn, and no tickets off.'

'I understand.'

'Look at me. You see I hold a stick that I've been whittling. Not out of ornament, I tell you, but for use. Now rack your brains for a reason.'

'To lick me with,' said the girl.

'Hit it, Six hundred and seventeen. If you tear, break, or waste anything, this stick will be a paintbrush to your back, making you like an ancient Briton, blue and yellow. Now look at this stick. You don't suppose I whittle and shape it for such as you; you ain't worth the exertion.'

'You thought me worth ten bob, or you wouldn't have given it,' said the child.

'You worth ten shillings!' sneered the Jew; 'not a bit. Your mother gave her gold ring as well; that was worth six.'

'Well, then, I'm valued at four.'

'Four! You're worth nothing. I reckoned on your clothes and boots.'

'My boots are scat at the sides, and wore out at the soles. They are fit for nothing but making soup. My clothes are that dirty with mud and coals that they'll never wash clean again.'

'What, given to argufying, are you?' exclaimed the pawnbroker. 'No more of that with me. Hook up the steps, if you please, you blackbeetle. I must find you a change somehow.'

He made her ascend a set of dark steps

into an upper story. There they went through three rooms, full as they could hold of various goods, old furniture, clocks, china, mattresses, looking-glasses, military accoutrements, uniforms, muffs, jackets, gowns, nautical instruments, books, tools.

'There,' said he, pointing above him with his stick, 'you see all these garments. This is the uniform of a general, that of an admiral. Here are sable and sealskin jackets, rabbitskin ermine opera cloaks, silk dresses for servant maids, and cotton prints for ladies, linen jackets of dockmen, worsted jerseys of sailors. These must all be hung on yokes. They accumulate. Unless exposed they don't attract attention. I fashion the yokes and pegs on which they hang. That is what I was whittling at. I always have one in hand. I have one great enemy with which to battle. These clothes don't eat, but they get eaten. The moth is my enemy. I said he was a great one, but really he's a very little one. Bless me! what valuable time is wasted at whack, whack, whack! with a bamboo to drive the moth out of the cloth and fur. I've tried camphor; I've tried bitter apple; I've tried pepper. Nothing answers but the bamboo. Now you know what will be one of your regular duties—duties! pleasures, exercises. You will have to beat the clothes every day for a couple of hours. If after this I find a moth I'll beat you, whack, whack, whack, with the bamboo, till I've beat the laziness out of you. You are intelligent. You can understand plain English, I suppose?'

Joanna nodded.

'You will have to work hard in this house,' said Mr. Lazarus further. He had beaten a carpet to illustrate his meaning, and raised a cloud of dust that made him cough. 'No idleness is tolerated here. No spare hours are given during which you may slip into mischief. Not much food to fire the blood and make you want it. You will rise at five and get me a cup of coffee. No lighting of fires, mind. The coffee is made in an Etna. Then you beat the clothes in the back yard till the shop opens. About noon the fire is kindled and dinner is cooked for me. You can eat what I leave. There is often gravy in which to sop bread. Gravy is nourishing. I don't consume it all myself. I am not greedy. Children only are greedy. In the afternoon you mind the shop, and mend what clothes are torn. About five o'clock I shall want a cup of tea. I take bread

and cheese for supper at nine. My teeth are
bad. I don't eat the crusts and rinds ; you may
have them, and be grateful. There are many
poor children with less. I had forgotten. You
must have a change of clothes.' He looked care-
fully about among the female garments. 'There,'
said he, ' I don't think I could dispose of these
traps ; they are much worn. I bought 'em
cheap ; came off a girl as died of scarlet fever.
Look sharp ; go behind a heap of furniture, off
with your wet and coaly rags, and tumble into
these beauties. Then, if you like, you may
wash your face and hands at the pump. Water
costs no money. I allow no soap.'

Joanna did not take many minutes in changing. She went into the back yard—this house
had one—and soused her head and arms well.
Then she returned with the utmost promptitude
to her master.

'I couldn't find a comb,' she said, 'so I
used a broken kitchen fork.'

'That's right,' answered the Jew approvingly ; 'never ask for two things when one
will suffice.'

Mr. Lazarus relaxed into amiability. He
was pleased with the ready instinct of the child
to meet his views.

'Let me tell you,' he said, 'when you've been a good girl, and worked hard and eaten next to nothing, I'll allow you, as a treat, to put on the general's uniform, sword, epaulette, and all ; or the admiral's, with his cocked hat; or my lady's silk and ermine, bare arms and low body. It will be as good as going to the play, and it will air the suits also, and prevent them getting mouldy.'

Joanna clapped her hands and laughed.

'There is one thing further' said Lazarus. 'You'll have to go to bed in the dark, winter and summer. I never allow waste of candle. Who knows? you might take to reading in bed —under the counter—and set everything in a blaze. Why, bless me ! if this establishment caught, the fire would run through it. Nothing in the world would arrest the flames. Now you may go down-stairs. No—stay. There is one point more to particularise. I spend a penny every week in getting shaved, and four-pence a quarter in having my hair cut. That amounts to five-and-fourpence in the twelve-month—clear waste, nothing to show for it. You will have to learn to shave me and cut my hair. Here is an old muff that the moth has played the mischief with. I don't think it will sell.

Practise on that. Lather it first, and then
work along it gently with a razor. You'll soon
get into the way, and save me five-and-four per
annum. Only—mind! Don't waste the soap!'

.   .   .   .   .

In all the many years that Emmanuel
Lazarus had done business he had never made
so good a bargain as when he took Joanna in
pawn. Ten shillings! She was worth to him
over ten pounds a year, that is two thousand
per cent. interest. He soon discovered her
worth, and congratulated himself on having
secured her.

Joanna worked from grey dawn to late at
night harder than any day-labourer. She slept
under the counter, and slept so lightly that
at the least alarm of burglars she woke and
screamed loud enough to scare away the rogues,
arouse the neighbours, and collect the police.

She dusted the weevils out of their lurking-
places; not a grub could conceal itself under
the felling; the bamboo reduced it to pulp.
Not a moth could spread wing; it was clapped
to dust between her palms. Wherever, in
cloth, dress, or fur cloak, she spied a rent, her
dexterous needle mended it so neatly that it
remained unperceived by purchasers. She

never forgot to lock the doors, bar and bell the windows, at night. Her clothing cost nothing, and was always neat, so well was it washed, so neatly was it mended, darned and patched. As she was denied coals, she washed the house linen and her own garments in cold water.

When winter set in, Joanna found means of economising that had not entered the brain of Lazarus. Charitable people had instituted a soup-kitchen. The girl had gone thither with her mother in their abject poverty. She went there now clothed in rags, and brought away sufficient nourishing broth to form the staple of her own and her master's dinner. Some potatoes and bread completed the meal. No one supposed that the wretched girl with worn face and appealing eyes was the maid-of-all-work to the rich Jew pawnbroker and money-lender of the Barbican.

Joanna had dark hair and large shining dark eyes too big for her face; the face was thin and sharp, but well cut. She was but twelve years old, therefore only a child; but the face was full of precocious shrewdness. The eyes twinkled, gleamed, flashed. Wonderful eyes, knowing eyes, without softness in them; eyes that saw everything, measured and

valued everything, that went into those she encountered and found out their weakness. Her
face was without colour, but the skin was clear
and transparent.

'Who and what are you, my child?' asked
a charitable woman once at the soup-kitchen.

'I'm a pawn—Six hundred and seventeen!'
she replied, and disappeared.

CHAPTER IV.

JOANNA'S SCHOOL.

SEVEN months after Joanna had been left in pawn with Mr. Lazarus, the Yorkshire skipper was again in Plymouth with a load of coals from Goole. He came to the shop to see the girl, and tell her about her mother. Captain Hull—that was his name—had bad news to communicate. Mrs. Rosevere had probably caught cold from her immersion, when she tried to drown herself, and on her voyage northward had been taken ill. On reaching Goole, she was carried on shore and sent to the nearest hospital, where she had been pronounced ill with rheumatic fever.

After that Mr. Hull had been to Belgium for iron. There had been a strike at Middlesborough, and the furnaces had been let out, and the ironmasters had executed their contracts by purchasing their iron at Verviers.

When next Captain Hull came to Goole and inquired after the woman, he learned that she had been discharged, but whither she had gone, and what was her present address, he was unable to ascertain. Joanna was much troubled. She had a tender spot in her heart. She was passionately devoted to her mother. Not a line had reached her from Mrs. Rosevere. Whether she were alive or dead she could not tell. She cried bitterly at night under the counter, and could not sleep for sobs. But she did not allow the skipper to see her tears. She shook and turned white when he told his tale, and then fled to the kitchen to conceal her emotion.

'Ah!' said the pawnbroker, when she had disappeared, 'this is my fate. I advanced ten shillings on the child, and now she is thrown on my hands. This is the second time this sort of thing has occurred—before it was white mice.'

'What about the white mice?'

'I advanced money on a couple of white mice to a schoolboy, and was not repaid. I had to feed those mice for weeks, and they cost me a fortune. I put them in the window, but, though it brought all the Barbican children to the glass, there came no buyer. At last I was forced to drown them, to be rid of the daily burden of their maintenance. The law won't let me deal like that with children. I'll never advance money on live animals again—never. I've been bitten twice, once by the mice, now by the girl. Ten shillings! I gave a half-sovereign in gold. I shall never see the colour of the coin again.'

'Now, Mr. Lazarus, speak nobut the truth. You gave ne'er a penny in cash. It was all took out in clothes.'

'Was it? Dear me, I had forgot. Well, it does not matter. I made a bad bargain. The creature eats with a voracity perfectly appalling. Did you ever see a cow or a horse in a meadow, how it goes on, never stopping? It is just the same with this child. The cost of her food is frightful, the cost of her clothes sickening. She outgrows her dresses as fast as they are fitted on her. Why did I take her? Why was I such a fool? This is what comes of having a feeling heart. Take her away, Mr. Hull, take her away, chuck her as ballast into the bilge-water in your hold. I've had her seven months, now it is your turn.'

I—I!' stammered the good-natured skipper, 'I am nae responsible for t' little lass.'

'You are. You sent her here. You persuaded the mother to put her with me, and offered her a place in your vessel. As you took the mother, you're part bound for the child. Now I've had enough of her gorging herself on butcher's meat, and swilling bottled ale, and burning candles at both ends, and flaunting in silks and satins.'

'None so much o' t' latter, I take it, Mr. Lazarus.'

'Only on Sundays, I allow. But, consider, Mr. Hull, a child can neither be clothed *in* nor *on* nothing. You, by the cut of you, I take to be a married man, and know what the cost of dressing children comes to.'

'This is but one bairn.'

'I know that; but this child is a girl, and girls cost more in clothes than boys.'

'Shoo works for you.'

'Works! Not she—loiters about the Barbican playing with the boys and girls at hopscotch and prisoners' base. Works! I've paid for her schooling.'

'Does she go to t' National school?'

'National school!' jeered the Jew. 'A

first-rate private school. She is slow at learning. I wish I could extract from her sufficient work to pay for her schooling. Take her away. I'll turn her out of doors if you don't. Not under half-a-sovereign would I consent to retain her.'

Mr. Hull considered for a while, then thrust his hand into his pocket and drew forth some money. 'If this be but a matter o' brass,' he said, 'take it. But I tell thee, I don't acknowledge the responsibility.'

'Very well,' said the Jew, 'I've a feeling heart, and I accept the trifle. It don't cover her breakages. I had as beautiful a pair of Oriental jars as you might wish to see. They were worth fifty pounds. The child knocked one over with a broom. What did she have a broom in her hand for? Cobwebs! Cobwebs don't hurt. Spiders break no china. Brooms does. Now there is but one jar remaining, and that is worth seven-and-six, because the pair is broken. That is a loss to a poor man. Take seven-and-six from fifty pounds, and it leaves forty-nine pounds twelve-and-six. You wouldn't like to lose forty-nine pounds twelve-and-six of a morning, would you, Mr. Hull? You see what sacrifices one makes through having a feeling heart. Mr. Hull, I'll take the money,

and set it off against the breakages : you contribute ten shillings and I forty-nine pounds
twelve-and-six.'

Mr. Hull grew red, and fumbled in his
pocket. 'Dang it!' said he, 'here's another
half-sovereign.'

'Thank you, captain, thank you. You
understand, it don't release her from pawn. The
mother pawned her, and has the ticket.'

'Oh, I don't want t' bairn out. Keep her
till her mother redeems her. I'm a'most feared
though t' old lass is dead. Shoo were but a
weakly creetur' at best.'

'I'll keep her till then,' said Lazarus, and
added to himself, 'I wouldn't do without her
for five-and-twenty pounds.'

As Mr. Lazarus said, Joanna was at school,
and the school was the private establishment of
Mr. Lazarus, in which he was head and second
master and usher rolled into one, and in which
she was the only scholar. Consequently on her
was concentrated the full teaching power of the
academy. She knew her letters and could sum
when she came there, but her knowledge of
men and the world was rudimentary. This was
the speciality of Mr. Lazarus's teaching. Under
his tuition she rapidly acquired an insight into

the shady ways of the world, and acquaintance with the skeletons in the cupboards of a good many houses in Plymouth.

Joanna also gained insight into her master's business, and unfolded a remarkable aptitude for it. The business was one that ramified in all directions, a fungous, cancerous growth with fibres extracting nutriment from every social bed.

Mr. Lazarus visited extravagant ladies at their homes, and lent them money on their diamonds. He gave out coppers on the flat-irons of drunken washerwomen. He took the gold repeaters of officers and the tools of artisans. He lent money on bills of sale, notes of hand, and post-obits. He was yielding about renewals.

The house was crowded from garret to cellar with articles of every description on which money had been advanced, or which had been seized in default of payment. A retentive memory was in demand to recollect where anything was, when wanted by a depositor, who came, money in hand, to release it; to know what pledges had lapsed, and when, without hunting them out of the ledger.

Dealers of various kinds visited Mr. Lazarus:

r. 2

slop-shop men to purchase a lot of secondhand
clothing, curiosity dealers to overhaul his china
and engravings, jewellers for his watches and
rings and bracelets, furniture-makers to buy up
cracked mahogany-veneered chests of drawers
for conversion into Florentine antiques by coat-
ing them with Dutch marquetry.

Thus the goods in Mr. Lazarus's establishment went into circulation. Old things went
and new came. But there always remained
some deposit which no tide swept away, and
which lay as a burden on the Jew's mind. The
articles occupied space and were unsaleable.
Joanna applied her mind to the solution of
this difficulty, and showed a rare sagacity in
converting them into usable, and therefore sale-
able goods, and thus launching them.

As Joanna grew up and grew into the business, she exhibited a rare talent in negotiating
with both sellers and purchasers. She did not
become the right hand of Lazarus, only because he had no right hand. Even he, with
his long experience, was unable to surpass her
in disparagement of articles offered, in shaming
a poor pledger into yielding them for a trifle.
The expressions she threw into her face, the
scorn that quivered in her finger-tips, the keen-

ness of eyesight that overlooked no defect, cowed the spirit of the pledger, and took the value out of the piece of goods before a word was spoken. On the other hand, in treating with dealers, her genius was equally conspicuous. She praised the articles, dexterously disguised their defects, flattered and cajoled the purchasers, and sent them away to find that they had been overreached. But what delighted Joanna especially was to have to do with an amateur antiquary or china fancier: then she became simplicity itself, profoundly ignorant of the real value of rare articles, and she sent the greenhorns off deluding themselves that they had secured treasures 'in a poky out-of-the-way odds-and-ends shop,' when they had paid heavy gold for utter rubbish.

Joanna, as has been said, developed admirable skill in turning unsaleable goods into articles of commerce. We give one instance. Mr. Lazarus was unable to resist the temptation of purchasing, at a low figure, a large number of scarlet uniforms slightly damaged and discoloured. No one would buy the red-cloth jackets. Joanna unpicked them, sent them into the dye vat, and with a pair of scissors and a needle and black thread converted them into fashionable short coats. The breast of one made the tail of another.

The demand for Mr. Lazarus's Rinking, Lorne, and Brighton suits, at a price with which the ready-made dealers could not compete, soon exceeded the supply.

When one of H.M.'s vessels was put in commission the mess was furnished with new linen, plate, china, glass. When discharged— sometimes at the end of a few months—everything was sold off at miserably low prices. Mr. Lazarus was a large and constant purchaser at these sales. Sometimes he took the entire lot in a lump, by negotiation, without auction. Then he and Joanna went over all the acquisitions with care. The markings were removed from the linen. If the table-cloths were much cut, they were converted into napkins ; if slightly injured, Joanna darned and disguised the cuts. The plate was subjected to much polishing, till it bore the appearance of new, or was redipped and sold as new—possibly to the same vessel when recommissioned. The glass was sorted into complete lots ; the knives and china found their way among the poor.

In their views of life Joanna and her master agreed perfectly ; but then Joanna's mind had been formed by Mr. Lazarus, and she drank in his doctrines as freely as he let her drink water.

Mr. Lazarus was a conscientious man in a way. He instructed Joanna in morals. He taught her that great sin would lie at her door if she acted towards himself dishonestly, and untruthfully and wastefully.

They had ample opportunity for exchanging ideas whilst feather-picking.

The pawnbroker received many pillows and bed-tyes as pledges. When he did so he slit them at a seam, put in his hand and extracted feathers; from a pillow he withdrew one handful, from a bed four. In their place he put hay, so as not to alter their weight. Then Joanna sewed up the seams so neatly that it could not be told they had been opened; and the feathers were stored in chests to be sold at tenpence per pound. Whilst thus engaged Joanna and her master discussed the world, the profligacy of the rich, the meanness of the poor, the greed of rival pawnbrokers, the universal corruption of men and morals.

What was the world coming to, when debtors bolted to America, and when those on whose furniture Mr. Lazarus had made advances 'flitted' by moonlight, leaving him out of pocket, without power of recovery? What was the world coming to, when the police poked their noses into his shop, and found there stolen goods, which they carried off, in spite of his having paid hard cash for them, or were extortionate in their demand for palm-greasing, to overlook the purchases? What was the world coming to, when charitable institutions were allowed to come to the aid of the distressed — clothing-clubs, coal-clubs, savings' banks—and hold them back from flying to their proper refuge, the Golden Balls? What was the world coming to, when the Jews were becoming so numerous and so unscrupulous as to interfere with one another's business? And what was the world coming to, when Gentiles were becoming a match for Jews in plucking the geese, and shearing the silly sheep, that asked to be plucked and shorn?

Thus Joanna grew up under this schooling, and the teaching became the grain of her mind. There was natural aptitude to receive it, but the aptitude was that of an active, eager, intelligent mind, ready to assimilate any instruction given it, with daily opportunity for testing and exercising it.

She was entirely without sympathy with her fellows. She looked upon men as the prey on which the clever lived; they were fair game when brought within reach through necessity or imbecility. Of human nature she had a low opinion, but she was brought into contact with no noble specimens.

Lazarus was without tenderness towards her; she grew up with no one to love, no one to love her, consequently there was no sympathy, pity, softness about her. The one leading motive of Lazarus's life seemed to be Individualism. He thought, worked only for himself. He concerned himself about no one; he was indifferent to the sufferings of mankind. His code of ethics was based on self. That was right which did him good, that was wrong which did him harm. He insisted to Joanna that the secret of success lay in rigidly attending to self-interest; that the failures of men were due to their yielding to their good-nature, to their vibration between self-interest and the care for others.

Thus passed several years. Joanna grew in stature, and her mind accommodated itself to what was exacted of it. She became indispensable to her master, but he was too shrewd to let her see how highly he appreciated her. No further news reached the Barbican about her mother. The skipper no more returned to Plymouth.

Still Joanna clung to the belief that her mother lived, and would return and redeem her before the lapse of the seven years.

CHAPTER V.

CRUDGE, SOLICITOR.

ONE evening, after Mr. Lazarus had shut up shop, his private door-bell was wrung sharply. Joanna answered it, but opened only so much of the door as allowed a portion of her face to appear, whilst she inquired the name and business of the visitor at so unwonted an hour.

'Crudge,' answered the caller; 'Crudge, solicitor. Come, open, and let me in. Here is my card.'

'Crudge, is it?' exclaimed Lazarus, who was behind the girl. 'Let in Mr. Crudge, Joanna, and don't keep him there under the drip of the door. Can't you see that it is raining, and that he has on his best hat? Joanna, be careful, lock and chain after the gentleman.'

Lazarus backed, bowing before his visitor, till he backed against a wall; then he stood hesitating, looking about him, doubtful whither to conduct Mr. Crudge.

'Really, sir,' said the Jew, 'I am sorry to
see you in so unworthy a den; but a shop is
not the rose-garden of Gulistan, and the seat
of business is not the lap of luxury. Where
shall we go? Will you condescend to step
into the kitchen?'

'Anywhere you like,' answered the lawyer.
'No ceremony with me. Give me a chair to
sit on, and a light by which to find one. I
want no more.'

'There is a nice easy arm-chair, leather
covered, with springs in the seat; but it is up-
stairs. It would take a quarter of an hour
to get it down. Besides, Inchball's 'British
Theatre,' in twenty-five vols. half-bound, the
rest in paper parts, occupy the seat. Time,
Mr. Crudge, is too precious a commodity with
you to let us think of that thin buoyant-seated
chair.'

'I will content myself with one that is
cane-bottomed,' said Mr. Crudge.

'I'm afraid I must ask you to take one
that *was* cane-bottomed, but is now sat through,
but will be re-caned in a fortnight,' said the
Jew apologetically. 'If you don't mind taking
a place between the præterite and the future
tenses, nothing can be better. It is not so far

gone that you will slip through. I will put a baking-tray from the oven over the hole, and then you will run no risk. Don't be afraid of grease. Nothing fatty ever goes into my oven. If you shirk it, take the dustpan.'

Mr. Crudge did not, however, relish the appearance of the chair offered him, or the kitchen into which he was introduced. He remained standing. Joanna entered after barring the door.

'I want to see you in private,' he said; 'I have come on business. We may need a table, and pens and ink. Besides,' he added, 'the place is full of feathers, and I don't want my coat covered with down.'

Mr. Lazarus laughed. 'Joanna has been plucking geese. Roast goose for dinner to-morrow. I would invite you to partake, Mr. Crudge, but your time is precious, and my house ill-suited as a place of entertainment. Plenty of goose-plucking done in this establishment, my dear sir, I assure you.'

No goose was visible, not even a fowl, but bolsters and pillows strewed the floor, and Mr. Crudge had to step over them by the light of a tallow candle stuck in the neck of a broken brandy bottle.

'If I might be allowed to propose,' said Lazarus, 'I would suggest your following me into my sanctum sanctorum. There we can talk together alone. Not that Joanna is to be considered. Step this way, Mr. Crudge. Joanna, let me have the light. You must sit in the dark, and pluck the goose after the gentleman is gone. Take care, Mr. Crudge, solicitor, there is a broken slate in the floor. Kick that bolster aside, it lies in your way. Don't strike your head against this butcher's steel-yard. Mind the floor; there is a dozen of mineral water ranged along the wall. You may notice an unpleasant savour. It is occasioned by nothing more than a dead rat. Overrun with them; so near the water; and I have poisoned them. They die in their holes, and under floors and behind wainscots. In a fortnight the smell will be gone. Here, sir, is my little room. You will excuse the bed being in it. Here is a seat for you, Mr. Crudge. It may be peculiar, but it is not uncomfortable. In fact, it is an old sedan-chair with the front knocked out. If you will look round the room you will see sedan-chairs let in between the presses. I got a stock of them, when they went out of fashion, and lay rotting in a yard.

They came in handy, fitted with shelves for keeping sundries, my papers, and poor valuables. One I use as a chair. I sit on it at the table. The sides cut off draughts. I'll turn it round. I can seat myself on the bed, if you will condescend to occupy the sedan-chair.'

Mr. Crudge looked about him. The room was small, lighted by day through a window, half of which was blocked up. Under the window was a table strewn with strips of paper, numbered—tickets to be affixed to pledges. Ink was in a broken liqueur-glass stuck into a cup full of shot. In an old dirty marmalade-pot was paste, and a brush. The paste was sour and watery. Against the wall on one side was a bedstead with a straw mattress on it, and a feather-bed to which hung a ticket. The bolster was labelled 145, the coverlet 374. Probably there were tickets to the blankets, but these Mr. Crudge did not see. Apparently no sheets were on the bed. Out of economy Lazarus used pledged goods; it saved the wear of what was his own. In the recesses on each side of the chimney were sedan-chairs, converted into cupboards. One was filled with bottles—laudanum, ipecacuanha, castor-oil, &c.

'Ah!' said Lazarus, marking the direction of his guest's eye. 'That was a bad bargain. Never able to dispose of this lot. Taken from a chemist. If either Joanna or I had been ill, and could have used some of them, the loss would not have been so dead. I keep 'em here, safe, as some of the lot may be poison.'

On the tops of the presses and sedan-chairs were boots, bottles, and crockery. On the chimneypiece were Chelsea figures. On a stool beside the table lay a scrap of newspaper, in which were a couple of onions and some salt.

Mr. Lazarus put the candle on the table, turned the chair about, and insisted on ensconcing the solicitor in it. Then he seated himself on the bed opposite his visitor.

Mr. Crudge was a tall, well-dressed man, of middle age, with reddish-brown hair. He wore whiskers and a moustache, but had his chin and jaw shaven below the moustache. He had grey eyes and a pair of bushy reddish eyebrows. His face expressed intelligence without imagination; it was a strong, practical, business face. His manner was that of a gentleman, easy and possessed. He took his place in the sedan-chair without a twitch of the muscles of his mouth. He was as insensible to the ludicrous as he was to poetry. Yet the situation was eminently grotesque. The sedan-chair had a roof and glass windows at the sides. It was open only in front, and Mr. Crudge was planted, as in a sentry-box, face to face with the Jew, sitting on the bed, with his legs folded like those of a Turk.

'Now,' said Mr. Lazarus, 'let us proceed to business. Something of importance must have occurred to bring you here at such a time.'

'Not at all,' answered Mr. Crudge. 'Nothing of vital importance that I am aware.'

'Then why have you come?' exclaimed Lazarus, dropping his legs over the side of the bed. 'Surely a letter would have sufficed. I could have run up to town to see you. You have travelled first class ; I would have gone third. You are not going to charge me for your time and trainage ? '

'Make yourself easy,' said the lawyer. 'I had to come to Plymouth on other business than yours, and as I was here, I thought best to give you a call at a time when I knew you would be disengaged. I am staying at the Royal. I did my business during the afternoon, had my dinner, and then strolled down here.'

Lazarus breathed freely. 'You gave me a

scare,' he said. 'What an expense I should
have been put to! Staying at the Royal!
wouldn't a commercial inn have done as well?
However, the other client pays, so it does not
matter.'

'Not at all to you,' said Mr. Crudge with
composure. 'I know your idiosyncrasies, and
accommodate myself to them.'

'Quite so. When you act for bloated pluto-
crats, make them pay. Letting off blood does
them good. When you act for poor hard-working labourers like myself, cut the expenses down.
Our blood is watery.'

'Enough on a topic that leads to nothing,'
said Mr. Crudge. 'You can guess what has
brought me hither.'

'I am afraid to guess. Is it the affairs of the
Duke?'

Crudge nodded.

'How do matters stand?'

'That depends on the point of view from
which the *coup d'œil* is taken. From yours,
excellent; from theirs, desperate. The family
are constantly in want of money—renewing,
mortgaging, and there must be a crash shortly.
Now they want about five thousand towards
finishing them.'

'Finishing them! Finishing for ever the great Kingsbridge family! Breaking down his most noble and exalted mightiness the Marquess of Saltcombe! Sweeping away, clearing away, and utterly effacing'—he jumped off the bed, and with the tail of his dirty coat brushed the table—' clearing away and utterly effacing the most gracious and ancient Eveleighs!'

'Mr. Lazarus,' said the solicitor coldly, craning his neck out of the box to watch the proceedings of the pawnbroker, ' pray observe that you have upset the ink and paste over the table in your effort to clean it. Instead of mending, you have messed the table.'

'I do not care. My fancy ran away with me. I am an Oriental, a child of the sun, with a rich imagination that flashes into poetry. What care I about these noble mushrooms? They date from the Conquest, but what is the Conquest to us? An affair of yesterday. I have done. Go on. They want more money, do they?' He reascended the bed, and sat on it with legs depending over the side.

'The end must come; it is inevitable,' said the solicitor. 'Everything is in your hands. You may bring the walls about their ears when you will. If you choose we can proceed to

F 2

extremities at once.   Nothing can save them.
You are practically the sole creditor, for you
have got the home mortgages into your own
hands.   You have no rivals to contend against.
The estate must be sold, and if you choose to
become possessor of Court Royal you may.'

Lazarus rubbed his hands, and crowed, rather
than laughed.

'I—I have the estates !   What good would
they do to me ?   I set up as a grand English
squire !   Not I.   That is not my ambition.   I
have Court Royal !   I could not keep it up.'

'Well, there is no accounting for tastes.   For
the *coup de grâce* we must have five thousand
pounds.   As usual, I suppose, the money is to
go through a third party, so that your name
may not appear ?   I will manage that.   I suppose some debts are pressing, and the usual
annual expense is becoming burdensome—that
is the occasion of this fresh demand.'

'Mr. Crudge,' said the Jew, 'you seem con-
fident that the end is near.   I do not share
your confidence.   A great house like that of
the Duke of Kingsbridge will not go to pieces
all at once.   It has its supports, on all sides, in
rich and powerful families.   When the rumour
spreads that the Kingsbridge house is trembling,

the noble relations from all parts will hasten to uphold it. There are a thousand means to which such a family may have recourse, inaccessible to such as us. They are like a tent pegged all round into the soil, and if this or that guy snaps what does it matter?—the rest will hold.'

' Who are to help them? The central pole of your tent is sawn through, and the guys will not uphold a fallen and flapping mass of rag. They stay it while upright, but are worthless when it is down.'

' But the house is not down yet. Why, Lord Edward is rector of a fat Somersetshire living, an archdeacon, and Canon of Glastonbury.'

' He may be worth some twelve hundred at the outside. He cannot help. Besides, he is already in debt. Lord Ronald, the general, has only his half pay.'

' But the family of the late Duchess ? '

' They will do nothing. However, I do not see in what way their fall can concern you, so long as you save your shekels. Whether the survivors of the wreck come to land or sink—that is nothing to you or me.'

' Nothing to me ! ' exclaimed the Jew, jumping off the bed and pacing the room. 'Nothing to me! It is everything to me. What do I care for money except as a means whereby I may lever them over, and throw them in the dirt under my feet?' He stopped abruptly, thinking he had said too much, and looked at the solicitor out of the corners of his eyes; but Mr. Crudge was leaning back in the sedan-chair, and Lazarus could see only his profile in shadow through the glass side.

'You speak as though you entertained a spite against the family,' he said—'as though you were moving in this matter, actuated by revenge for some personal wrong. But that is impossible. What can you, the mole that burrows at the root of the social tree, have against the purple emperor butterfly who flutters about its very top on shining wing? The distance between you is too great for you ever to have come in contact.'

'To be sure, I have expressed myself over-strongly. My feeling is not personal, it is political.'

'Oh!' said the lawyer. 'Now I understand.'

'Of course you understand. Political feelings fire the passions as surely as personal wrongs.'

'To be sure they do,' said Crudge, with indifference.

After a pause, Lazarus got off his bed and said, ' If five thousand more is necessary, you shall have the sum. I have waded too deep into the morass to think of retreat; I must wade on. Tell me candidly: in your opinion, is there no salvation for them ? '

' That I will not say. There is a desperate resource. The Marquess may marry an heiress, and with her fortune disencumber the property.'

' He is capable of doing it,' cried Lazarus in great excitement. ' He will do it; curses be upon him ! Why, any American plutocrat, or Liverpool merchant, or London corn-factor would throw his millions into the Kingsbridge chat-moss to make a way over it for his daughter to win a coronet. The Marquess is only forty, is a handsome man—that will be the checkmate they will play ! '

' The Marquess is forty, as you say, or thereabouts. He has been languidly looking out for heiresses these ten years, but heiresses don't fly into your mouth like roast partridges in the land of Cockaigne. He must stalk them. He must make efforts to find them. However, that is no concern of mine. All I have to look to is your pecuniary interest in the Kingsbridge estates.'

'Five thousand will nigh upon finish them up, will it?' said the Jew. 'They take a deal of finishing, like a painting by Meissonier. I thought the last loan would have done that. What is the property worth? Have you an idea? What are the old mortgages on the other estates?'

'That is more than I can say. I know what is owing to you. You have the mortgage on the manor of Court Royal, the sun and centre of the whole system.'

Lazarus considered, then drew a key from his pocket, opened an iron box walled into the side of the house, and drew from it an account-book and his cheque-book.

'Now,' said Mr. Crudge, 'see the result of getting excited. You upset the ink, and now you want to use it.'

'If you do not mind being left a moment in the dark, I will fetch some ink,' answered the Jew. 'I see that what lies on the table is useless; it is a flux of coalash, ink, and paste; a picture of our social system, eh, Mr. Crudge! —a mixture of messes.'

Lazarus withdrew with the candle.

Mr. Crudge sat back in his chair and crossed his legs. A very little grey light stole in through the upper part of the window.

'Bah!' said he to himself. 'This sort of people object to fresh air. What with the onions, and the sour paste, and the dead rats, and the pervading Levitical savour, I am asphyxiated. No washing apparatus in the room, I perceive. I should have perceived it without a light.' Then he heard soft steps approach. The door was thrown open and feet entered the room. In another moment a match was struck and flared. Mr. Crudge, who had turned his head, saw through the window of the sedanchair that the girl stood in the room. Joanna came forward and held the match before his face, studying him intently. She said nothing. Mr. Crudge was too surprised to speak. He looked at her. She was a girl of about seventeen, tall, slightly built, with olive complexion, very dark hair, and large shrewd eyes. The match flame repeated itself in them as red stars. She had outgrown her garments, which were too tight and too short. Her arms were bare. She was in her stocking-soles. Her lips were compressed; she remained immovable till the

match burnt to her fingers ; then, instead of
throwing the red end on the ground, she extinguished it in her mouth. She said not a
word, but turned in the dark and went away
as softly as she had come.

Presently Lazarus came back with the
candle in one hand and a bottle of ink in the
other.

' I could not remember where I had put it,'
he said ; ' at last I found the ink in the howdah.'

' In the what ? '

' There was an elephant brought over from
India for a showman a few years back, and the
howdah was brought over with it. Sixpence a
ride, children half price, would soon have re-
couped the howdah and the beast. But it was
not to be. It was to be dead loss. Such is life !
The elephant died on board ship, and the howdah was sold. I bought it, but have not yet
been able to dispose of it. Do you happen to
want a howdah ? '

' Certainly not ! '

' You needn't pay cash down,' said the Jew.
' You'd deduct the howdah from your bill.
Perhaps you'll consult your missus about it
when you get home.'

The Jew put candle and ink on the table.

'I've been considering,' he said, 'that it would be well for you to go down to Court Royal and have a look at the place and the people. Then you will be able to give me an account of how the land lies. I can't go myself; I have my loan office, as well as the shop, and I can't leave the girl to manage both.'

'A queer piece of goods she seems,' said the lawyer.

'That she is; queer here,' said the Jew, touching his head; 'an idle minx with an egregious appetite. Eats everything, even the candle-ends. But enough of her; she has nothing to do with Court Royal, and never will have. What do you say to my proposal?'

'I can't travel and spend valuable time without proper remuneration.'

'You shall be paid,' answered the Jew. 'I will not grudge a small sum in this instance. I shall be easier in my mind when you have been down to the place and taken stock of what is there. You see, I've had myself to lean on friends to find all the money I wanted; if they pay me—they at Court Royal—it is not all profit. I have to pay interest also for what I took up to help me to get hold of the main mortgages. There,' he continued, 'is the differ-

ence between us Jews and you Christians.   We
hang together like a swarm of bees, one holding
on by another; and you are like a hive of
wasps, stinging each other, and when one
gathers honey the other eats it, so that their
combs are always empty.   Will you go to Court
Royal?'

'I will.   Indeed, it is as well that I should
have a personal interview with the steward, as
the negotiations are carried on through him.'

'You will travel second class, not first,' entreated Lazarus.   'Money spent on the railway
in comfort is waste.   From Kingsbridge Road
there is a coach.   You will travel outside.   The
inside places are secured several days in advance.
If you return the next day you need not tip the
driver two shillings; eighteenpence will suffice.'

'Very well; I will go to morrow.'

CHAPTER VI.

THE DUCAL FAMILY.

In the afternoon of the next day the coach deposited Mr. Crudge at the principal inn of Kingsbridge, 'The Duke's Arms.' After depositing his valise and securing a room, he ordered a fly to take him to the steward, who, he ascertained, lived out of the town, near the park gates. 'An open carriage,' said Mr. Crudge; 'it don't seem likely to rain, and I like to look about me.'

The drive was not a long one, through a pleasant wooded vale, commanding glimpses of the inlet of sea, now that the tide was flowing, flushed with water. The hills and moors over which the coach had run from the station had been bare, and the contrast of the luxuriant vegetation and stately growth of trees in the hollows was therefore the more striking and agreeable.

The carriage drew up before a neat white house, with a green veranda, and roses and westeria trained over it. Here lived Mr. Christopher Worthivale, steward of the Duke of Kingsbridge.

A maid answered the bell, and informed Mr. Crudge that the steward was at home and disengaged. She showed him into a drawing-room which, though well furnished, looked as if it were never used. The walls were white, with gold sprigs; the carpet very green, the table cover and the covering of the chairs greener still. The window-curtains lace, stiff with starch, and smelling of it. On the wall, over the fireplace, was a proof engraving of his Grace, Beavis, seventh Duke of Kingsbridge; against the fireplace—there was no fire, and no appearance of there ever having been one—a banner screen of needlework, glazed, representing the ducal arms, with supporters and coronet. On the table was an album, containing photographs, at which Mr. Crudge looked whilst waiting. First came his Grace, in cabinet size; then one of Lord Edward, Rector of Sleepy Hollow, Canon of Glastonbury, and Archdeacon of Wellington; one of General Lord Ronald Eveleigh, K.C.B.; one of Lady

Grace Eveleigh, and one of the Marquess of Saltcombe. Then two blank pages, with places never occupied, and after that, at a respectful distance, photographs taken from faded daguerreotypes of the late Mr. and Mrs. Worthivale, parents of the present steward. The late Mr. Worthivale had been steward to the last, and penultimate, and the present Duke; a stout, grey-haired old gentleman, in a white beaver, with high collar, and a plaid waistcoat. The old gentleman had probably possessed blue eyes. They had not taken in the daguerreotype, and consequently had not reappeared in the carte, but both insisted emphatically on the plaid of the waistcoat, as if this was, taken all in all, the thing about Mr. Worthivale, senior, which demanded perpetuation. Judging from her photograph, Mrs. Worthivale must have been a cast-iron woman, in black silk that also looked like iron, with twisted iron wire for curls. After these portraits followed those of Mr. Christopher Worthivale; of his deceased wife, a sweet, patient-looking woman; of his son Beavis, called after the Duke, who had graciously condescended to stand godfather; and of his daughter Lucy. On a cabinet stood a beautiful carved alabaster vase, with swans,

forming the handles, drinking out of it, under
a glass bell. Into the pedestal of ebony was
let a silver plate, on which was engraved a
notice that this vase was presented to Mr.
Christopher Worthivale by his Grace, Beavis,
seventh Duke of Kingsbridge, G.C.B., as a
small testimonial of esteem, on the twenty-fifth
anniversary of his stewardship. Above this
hung a painting in oils, by a local artist, of
Court Royal ; and on each side of it a portrait,
also in oils, the one of a favourite horse of the
late Duke, the other of a favourite dog of the
late Dowager Duchess.

Mr. Christopher Worthivale entered, whilst
Mr. Crudge was studying these pictures. He
was a hale, fresh-coloured man of about five-
and-fifty, in a light grey coat and a white
waistcoat. He entered briskly, rubbing his
hands. Judging by his appearance and manner,
one would have supposed that the property
of the Duke was in a flourishing and unencum-
bered condition, and that the steward's manage-
ment of it had been most successful. Not a
shadow lay on his cheerful face. His manner
was perfectly easy. On his left-hand little
finger he wore a ring with a red cornelian, on
which were cut the three pheons of Worthivale

of Worthivale, an old respectable Cornish family which he claimed to represent.

'Allow me to introduce myself,' said Mr. Crudge. 'My name is familiar to you—Crudge, solicitor, Exeter. I have come on business about which we have had some correspondence.'

'Ah! Mr. Crudge, to be sure. The maid got hold of your name wrong. I did not anticipate the pleasure. Gooche was what she said. Pray take a seat. Neither your name nor business are strange to me. Mutual accommodation, eh? Do sit down. Really, I am delighted to see you. You could not have done me a greater pleasure.'

The expression of Mr. Worthivale's face belied his words. On hearing the name of his visitor some of his cheerfulness had faded from his countenance and his lips twitched.

'I entreat you to be seated,' he went on, nervously offering one chair, then another, then, noticing an arm-chair, rolling that up, then falling back on a fourth, a low light seat of *papier mâché*. 'You have come a long way. By coach? May I offer you refreshments?'

'Thank you, I will not take anything. My time is precious. If you have no objection, I would like at once to proceed to business.'

'Oh! business,' echoed Mr. Worthivale, taking out his pocket handkerchief, and dusting the books on the table. 'Dear me! how provoking the servants are. They take advantage of there being no lady in the house to neglect the primary obligations of domestic service. I cannot see to everything—his Grace's affairs and the dusting of my drawing-room. I beg your pardon, what was the business on which you wished to consult now?'

'That mortgage held by the Messrs. Stephens. It must be paid, I understand. It is called up. There is a little difficulty, I am led to suppose, some tightness——'

'Nothing to speak of, nothing at all,' interrupted the steward airily. 'Of course we can find the money. We can offer such excellent security, that it can always be got. You are certain you will take nothing? Not some claret?'

'Excuse me, I should like to settle this matter at once. I believe the interest has been falling in arrear. I have called on Messrs. Stephens. They do not wish any scandal; the sum is, comparatively, not large. All Messrs. Stephens want is their money, and I have a client who will advance it, the mortgage to be transferred to him.'

'That is exactly what I should propose,' said the steward, drawing a long breath. 'All we require to clear off these encumbrances is delay. A calling in of the sums standing on the estates would be inconvenient just at present. The seasons have been bad of late— five detestable years; several farms are thrown on our hands, and we have no tenants offering; others we have had to reduce to keep them occupied. The old-fashioned seasons must return eventually—a matter of time only. Then we shall be afloat again. That little sum about which I wrote—— ?'

'Five thousand. That will also be lent by my client on note of hand at five per cent.'

'Who is this client, may I ask?'

'A Mr. Emmanuel.'

'Emmanuel!' echoed the steward, moving uneasily on his chair. 'I must say I do not relish the idea of being so deeply indebted to Jews. Unfortunately we are already somewhat teased with them. The Marquess, when he was in the army, was rather reckless. It lasted a few years, and then he learned discretion; but when sowing wild oats he bought his grain of bad seedsmen.'

'Indeed, are the debts serious?'

'Oh, no! not at all—not for a marquess, heir to a ducal estate. We only want him to clear these off. Emmanuel! Who is this Emmanuel? He seems to be getting a much tighter grip on us than I like. First one thing, then another, goes to Mr. Emmanuel. You see this present mortgage is a very important one, it is on the manor of Kingsbridge. He holds that on Court Royal already. Who is this Emmanuel?'

'A client who wants safe investment in land. He is trustee to an orphan, and must put the money where it can be secure. What security better than his Grace's property?'

Mr. Worthivale considered a moment; then he said, 'You will allow me to talk the matter over first with the Marquess. You are aware, no doubt, that his Grace is getting on for eighty years, and unable to devote his attention to business—except quite subsidiary matters—partly on account of his advanced age, partly because he suffers from heart complaint, and must be spared excitement. The Marquess looks after things for him—that is, he is supposed to do so, and he does sometimes. I am in his confidence. Indeed, I am his most trusted adviser. I act for the best, always in the interests of the

family, but I consult the Marquess in everything, and he does me the honour, sometimes,
of listening to me, and quite devoting his mind
to what I suggest.'

Crudge nodded, but said nothing.

'Your time, I think you said, was precious.
You will probably be returning to Exeter to-
morrow?'

'To-morrow afternoon.'

'Then the business will have to be settled
as soon as may be. Let me see—— Have
you a dress coat with you?'

'In my portmanteau at the inn.'

Mr. Worthivale drew a sigh of relief.
'That simplifies matters. If you see no reason
against it, I will send a note up to the Marquess' (really it was down hill all the way to
Court Royal, nevertheless with Mr. Worthivale
it was *up*). 'I will ask if I may take you
there to dine to-night, quite *en famille*, you
understand. There are only Lord Ronald, and
Lord Edward, and the Vicar, and a neighbour
or two there. Half-past seven is the hour.
Will you return to Kingsbridge, and get on
your evening dress, and drive back? You can
come here, pick me up, and we will go on together. You are positive you have a dress

suit with you?—I couldn't, you understand—
without——'

'Set your mind at rest. I have dress
clothes with me.'

'I am so thankful to hear it; I thought it
possible you had not. When travelling on
business we don't always care to cumber ourselves with superfluous luggage, you understand.
To-day is his Grace's birthday, and Lord Edward
has come from Somersetshire to see the Duke
and to dine with him. Lord Ronald lives at
Court Royal. There are no others, but the
Vicar and a neighbouring squire or two. I
was invited as a devoted adherent to the family.
Very kind. Also my son Beavis, who has the
honour of being his Grace's godchild. My
daughter, Lucy, is companion to Lady Grace.
They were brought up together, and Lucy lives
at the Court. Dear me! Bless my soul!
The housemaid has left the duster in the room,
stuffed it under the fender, and thinks it out of
sight. As I am alive, there are the stove
brushes also. Under the circumstances, you
understand, if you had been without a dress
coat'—he looked down at Mr. Crudge's feet—
'and patent-leather boots?'

'I have slippers and red silk stockings.'

'They will do. Quite the thing. I feel so light of heart. You are supplied in every other particular? I should be so proud——?'

'I always take about with me paper collars, cuffs, and dickies.'

'Paper! Dickies!' echoed Mr. Worthivale. 'You will excuse me, I know—but I hardly like to—that is, I hardly think that—in a word, I would not for the world show any disrespect to his Grace, especially on his birthday. You see a duke stands at the very summit of the social scale—next to Royalty. Archbishops only go before by order of precedence, but that is a relic of pre-Reformation priestcraft which set the Church above the State. An archbishop may be any Jack or Tom. You will not take it amiss if I offer to lend you one of my shirts?'

'Not at all ; not at all.'

'And you will not fail to be here at seven?'

'I will not fail.'

Mr. Crudge, as a lawyer, was punctual. Precisely at seven his fly drew up at Mr. Worthivale's door, and the steward joined him.

'Do you see,' asked the steward, as a woman in a scarlet cloak opened the gates of the drive, 'all the females who appear in the grounds are expected to wear old-fashioned red cloth cloaks

and hoods?   His Grace supplies them at Christmas.   The effect is charming among the green
shrubs and on the shaven lawns.   Do look about
you at the trees.   Are not these araucarias
superb?   I believe these were the first planted
in England.   The mildness of the climate and
the fertility of the soil have made them thrive.
Look at the hydrangeas.   Did you ever see
anything like them?   Blue, all blue, owing to
the iron in the soil.   The rhododendron and
azalea season is the time to see this place to
perfection.   The two-mile drive between banks
of flowering shrubs is scarcely to be surpassed.
I should have liked to take you through the
vineries, orchard-houses, pinery, and conservatories.   The Duke and the Lady Grace are
passionately fond of flowers.   He grudges no
money on his gardens and glass-houses.   You
like this gravelled road, do you not?   We have
to send to the Tamar copper-mines for the
gravel.   It comes in barges from Morwellham
to Kingsbridge.   It is so charged with mundic
and arsenic as to poison the weeds for seven
years.   It comes rather costly, but there is no
gravel like it, a beautiful white spar.   His Grace
can endure no other gravel.   We have some six
miles of gravelled walks and drives done with

it in the park and gardens. You have a pair of gloves with you, I hope? I myself wear them until I enter the room, lest my fingers should get dirty. Are your hands moist? Hold them against the glass to cool them. I do not myself like shaking hands when my hands are warm. There, from this point you get a lovely glimpse of the estuary and the beautiful hills behind, with the tower of Stokenham on the height. It is too dark for you to distinguish the tower, but you can see the water. I call the creek an estuary, but, as a fact, no rivers run into it. The Avon flows away behind that bank of hill. There is the Court: a fine pile of buildings, is it not? all built of Yealmton limestone. I call it limestone, but, in fact, it is marble. By this light you cannot see how prettily it is veined. The late Duke began the mansion, and the present Duke completed it, about forty-three years ago. It is in the Doric order.'

'It must have cost a pot of money,' observed Mr. Crudge.

'It cost a great deal of money,' said the steward coldly. 'Dukes do not keep their money in pots, like old women.'

'Is it paid for?' asked the lawyer.

'Well——— It is rather unfortunate that
their Graces were obliged to build, but, really,
they could not help themselves. The old
house was Elizabethan, very suitable for a
country squire or for a baronet. I am not sure
that even a baron might not have put up with
it, but it was not of a scale—of a sort—it had
not the height' (Mr. Worthivale spread his
hands illustrative of its dimensions) 'you understand. A duke is a duke, and must be ducally
lodged. If you have a sun, you must have
a firmament to contain it. Even the dome
of St. Paul's would be ridiculous. You understand.'

The fly drew up under the Doric portico,
and the steward and his companion were
received into the house by men in the ducal
livery of buff and scarlet.

An expression of humility and of piety
diffused itself over the face of Mr. Worthivale
as he ascended the broad marble staircase,
thickly carpeted, towards the drawing-room.
Crudge was not oppressed nor surprised at
what he saw. He looked round him with
curiosity. The entrance-hall was stately, with
polished marble pillars and pilasters. It was
lighted by a chandelier. Beautiful paintings

adorned the walls. Footmen in buff and scarlet flitted about like moths on a hot day.

Mr. Worthivale whispered, ' Yonder is a Gainsborough, of Lady Selena Eveleigh, afterwards Countess of Grampound. This is a Rubens—splendid colouring. But you should see those at Kingsbridge House, Piccadilly. Pity they are so fleshy that really a curtain over them is needed. The subject of this I do not understand. It is allegorical. Hush ! here we are.'

They were conducted through the state drawing-room, which was lighted, but empty, into a smaller room, whence they heard the sound of voices. This was a charming boudoir, white and gold, with rose silk curtains and rose satin coverings to the sofas and chairs. In a large easy chair by the fire sat his Grace the Duke of Kingsbridge, a tall, white-haired, noble-looking man, with a high ivory forehead, a pale transparent complexion, caused by the disease from which he suffered, his eyes dark and piercing. His face was oval, his features finely modelled, the nose aquiline, but not so much as to give the idea of strength to his face. The face was refined, dignified, and cold. It wanted vigour, but was modelled with inflexible obstinacy.

Lord Ronald, the general, was like him, but richer in colour, and his features were bolder. He was erect, decided in his movements, and looked what he was, a soldier. His hair was grey, and he wore grey whiskers and moustache. Lord Edward, the Archdeacon of Wellington, was a smaller man than his brother, grey headed, with a sallow complexion, much wrinkled. His eyes were wanting in brilliancy, and his face bore an expression of nervous timidity. He had lost his front teeth, and this had altered the shape of his mouth, and given him a look less aristocratic than his brothers.

The Marquess of Saltcombe, who was also in the room, was a handsome man of about forty, with dark hair, dark eyes, and military moustache. The rest of his face was shaven. His eyes were fine, but wanting in fire; indeed, the general expression of his face lacked animation. He was grave, dignified, with a pleasant smile, which he put on when spoken to, but the smile never mounted to his face spontaneously. He had laughed without merriment, argued without enthusiasm, pitied without sympathy, and acted without impulse. He had been in the army, but had left it; not caring for political life he had not attempted to enter Parliament. He lived at home, was too inert to go to town, and entered without eagerness into country pursuits.

Other gentlemen were present, but Mr. Crudge did not notice them particularly. Among the ladies present the only one who was conspicuous was Lady Grace Eveleigh. the daughter of the Duke. She was tall, like the rest of the family, and had the family refinement and nobility of type; but to this was added great purity and sweetness, and a very gentle, almost pleading manner. Mr. Worthivale introduced the lawyer to the Marquess, who was nearest to the door, and was apparently expecting their arrival. Then Lord Saltcombe took on himself the task of introducing Mr. Crudge to his father and uncles and sister. The Duke slightly rose from his seat and bowed with courtesy, but without encouragement; Lord Edward held out his hand, and made some general remark, his kind face relaxing into a friendly expression. Lord Ronald shook hands and said a few words. The lawyer felt that, although he had moved in all sorts of society, he was as a fish out of water here. The brothers looked on him as a stranger from another sphere, whose presence must be tolerated, who would never rise even to the level of acquaintanceship. The Duke exchanged a few words with him on the weather, and the drive from the station, and on the prospect of a branch line being made to Kingsbridge, 'which,' said he, 'I shall oppose,' and then turned to the Vicar and Sir Edward Sheepwash, and continued with them a conversation which had been interrupted by the introduction of Mr. Crudge.

The Marquess and Worthivale engaged him in desultory talk, and after a while shook him off. Then Lady Grace, seeing that the lawyer looked ill at ease, drew towards him, and provoked a conversation as lively as was possible under the conditions of their having no points in common.

'Let me introduce you to my dearest friend, my almost sister, Miss Lucy Worthivale,' said Lady Grace; 'and perhaps you will take her in to dinner?'

Miss Worthivale was a pretty young lady with bright colour and large, soft, dark eyes. Her face brimmed with good-nature. It was, perhaps, a little flat and moon-shaped, but its

effect was sunny. Her eyes were everywhere.
Mr. Crudge saw that she was made useful in
the house in many ways to relieve Lady Grace
of irksome duties, and stand between her and
annoyances.

Crudge observed that her attention was
generally directed to Lady Grace, whom she
evidently admired and loved with her whole
soul. Lady Grace occasionally caught her
friend's eye during dinner, smiled, and then a
flush of pleasure kindled the honest face of
Lucy. Because his companion looked so much
towards the end of the table, the solicitor found
his eyes also wandering in the same direction.
Lady Grace was clearly not very young. Mr.
Crudge conjectured that her age was about
five-and-twenty; but though not a girl, her
pure face was luminous with the light of a
child's innocence. The complexion was trans-
parently white, with a little colour that came
and went as a flicker in her cheek, and yet it
was so faint and doubtful that it was difficult
to say whether what flickered there was colour
or a smile. There was something almost sad
and appealing to pity in her eye and mouth;
yet Lady Grace had known no sorrow, had met
with no contradiction. Her life had been un-

clouded and unvexed. Her mouth was flexible, fine, and tremulous; her voice soft, low, and sweet.

Mr. Crudge was a man utterly without idealism. He could read no poetry except Crabbe. Yet he could hardly withdraw his eyes from her face. She fascinated even the commonplace man of business. She puzzled him. He thought within his mind how he should get on with her if he had business transactions with her. Women's minds, as he believed, were made up of so much care about servants, so much about dress, so much solicitude about the goings on of their neighbours, a screwiness about money, a pinch of good nature, and a spice of spite, all stirred up together till well mixed. But there was nothing of this in the face before him. He shook his head; it was like the dish before him, made up of unknown ingredients.

Beside her on one side sat the Vicar, an elderly and gentlemanly man, with views like a rose of wax, to be moulded by any man who put his hand to it and thumbed it. He was so much of a gentleman that he would differ with no one. Next him sat a young man who was speaking to no one, and was only occasionally addressed by Lady Grace, who, with ready tact, saw that he was out of the conversation.

'That is my brother,' said Lucy, in answer to a query of the solicitor. 'There was no lady for him to take in to dinner. He has been in a lawyer's office. Papa thought it a good training for him. Of course he will be steward after papa. His Grace did us the favour of standing as his godfather. I fancy he would rather not have been here this evening, though he is quite at home in Court Royal, but my father pressed him to come.'

Crudge looked across at him with interest. Here, at all events, was a man who belonged to his world—who felt uncomfortable, out of place, in the sphere in which he found himself.

When the ladies withdrew, he moved his glass, so as to be opposite him and enter into conversation, but found the steward come up beside him and engage him.

'The Lady Grace,' said Mr. Worthivale, 'is very lovely. Do you not think so? We are all her worshippers here—from a distance, looking up at her as an unapproachable star.'

'A little *passée*, eh?'

'Not at all, not at all,' said Worthivale colouring. 'She is a most charming person.'

'I should suppose so,' answered the solicitor.

'And the Duke? You have had some conversation with him. I heard the weather and the branch spoken of. A commanding intellect. A most charming person; wonderful man for his age. Seventy-six to-day, and in full command of his faculties.'

'Obstinate, eh?'

'Not at all—firm,' said Worthivale with a frown. 'When he says a thing he sticks to it. You see that Lord Edward is a delicate man. He had not the physique of the rest, that was why he was put into the Church. Yet it was a pity, as his intellectual powers are considerable, and he might have done well in the diplomatic service. A most charming man. Lord Ronald is a fine old soldier; was in the Crimean war, where he distinguished himself. A man full of information on all military matters—perfectly charming. You have, I believe, had a chat or two with the Marquess; he is now talking to my son. They have known each other since boyhood, and there is almost the attachment of friendship between them— as far as friendship can subsist between two so

widely removed in the social scale. I hope
that eventually my son will succeed to the
stewardship. Of course he is young now, and
the affairs demand an old head——' He
paused, and moved uneasily. 'Altogether the
Marquess is a most charming man.'

'Quite so,' said Mr. Crudge.

'There is our Vicar,' pursued the steward.
'An agreeable person, but tiresome. To-morrow
he will dine with a gentleman of means, but no
birth, in the town, and be quite Liberal, if not
Radical, when his feet are beneath his maho-
gany. He leads a life of it; he is pulled this
way and that by the ladies of his congrega-
tion, who have their various and discordant
views.'

'That,' said Mr. Crudge, 'strikes me as the
weakness of the Church of England. She
is trying to balance herself between two stools,
a position neither dignified nor secure.'

'Still,' said the steward, 'with this abatement
he is a charming man.' Then he held up his
finger: 'His Grace is speaking.'

'I do not myself see how we can escape a
complete political and social revolution,' said
the Duke to the Vicar, Sir Edward Sheepwash,
and the Archdeacon of Wellington. 'If the

franchise is entrusted to the Have-nots, the Haves must go down. They must go down for this reason——'

'Which is the Ducal family?' whispered Crudge. 'Haves or Have-nots, or Have and Have-not in one?'

'Hush,' said Worthivale.

'They must go down for this reason, that the appeal to the electors will be an appeal to Cerberus, and Cerberus must be given cakes. Now, it is absurd to affect indignation against bribery and corruption in boroughs, and yet extend the franchise to the needy. If the needy have the franchise, you must appeal to their cupidity. It is the only appeal they can understand. The new class of electors are earthworms, all stomach. Whichever party desires to get into power must appeal to their cupidity, or for evermore stand out of power. Hitherto bribery has meant the candidate throwing away his own money; henceforth he will throw away that of others, and that will not be bribery. I bribe the electors of Kingsbridge if I allow them to shoot rabbits over my preserves. I do not bribe if I promise them the land of the aristocracy and the tithes of the Church.'

'Already,' said the Archdeacon, 'the farmers

are crying out that they are crushed by the rates.'

'Very well,' said the Duke ; let the Liberals go to the country with the offer of disestablishment and disendowment, the tithe to go to cover the rates and relieve the farmers, and you will see the farmers to a man will turn Radical.'

'If the Church were disestablished we should have to become definite,' said the Vicar, a white-haired, round, red-faced, good-natured man. 'I cannot imagine anything more disastrous to the Church than to become definite.'

'The House of Lords will never pass disestablishment,' said the Archdeacon.

'The House may go too,' said the Duke.

'The country is gone crazed,' said the General, ' or it would not have endured the short-service system. What should you say to those who trained men to be carpenters, or engineers, or lawyers, and, as soon as they had mastered their professions, told them to get about their business and take to something else ?'

The Duke sighed: 'I may not live to see it, but the House of Lords will go.'

'And with it the Church will fall,' said the Archdeacon.

'The army is gone to the dogs already,' said the General.

Mr. Crudge leaned across the table, and said to Beavis Worthivale: 'I see by the direction of your eyes you are trying to decipher an inscription over the chimney-piece that has been puzzling me. I am too shortsighted to read it from where I sit.'

'It is the motto of the family,' said the young man, ' written all over the house— " *Quod antiquatur et sene.cit, prope interitum est.*" '

'Scripture, eh?'

' Yes, Scripture. " That which decayeth and waxeth old is ready to vanish away." '

' Very good—very appropriate. " *Prope interitum est.*" '

CHAPTER VII.

BEAVIS.

' I REALLY think,' said Mr. Crudge, as he stood in the hall, being helped into his overcoat, and while the fly was at the door to take him to his inn—'I really think, as it is dry underfoot, that I will walk to Kingsbridge. The night is lovely, the moon is full, and I have a pair of goloshes in my greatcoat pocket.'

' I will accompany you, if you have no objection,' said Beavis Worthivale. ' I also would enjoy the walk. My father can return in your fly. He is without an overcoat, and he will not lock up till I reappear.'

' Is Miss Worthivale coming ? '

' Lucy? Oh, no! She lives at the Court, and only visits at the Lodge,' answered Mr. Worthivale. 'We see little of her. She is always with the Lady Grace.'

'If you are ready,' said Mr. Crudge to the young man, 'I am at your service.'

The night was indeed lovely. The moon hung unclouded over the sea, which gleamed in vistas opened among the trees of the park. Myrtles, magnolia, geraniums luxuriated in the warm, equable climate of the south coast, uncut by east winds, unchecked by late frosts. Above, the silver moon, walking in brightness; below, Mr. Crudge, walking in his goloshes. Mr. Crudge turned and looked back at Court Royal. The moon was on the front of the mansion. It was a noble pile of buildings, worthy of the residence of a duke. Behind rose hills covered with oak and beech woods, interspersed with Scottish fir and silver pines. In the moonlight. with the lighted windows, and the bank of park trees behind, it resembled a beautiful ivory sculpture, studded with golden points, reposing in a bed of black velvet.

But Mr. Crudge had no thought of the loveliness of the scene. 'To live in a place like this,' said he, 'and in this style, a man should have forty or fifty thousand, and the family have not that—clear. It is the poorest ducal house in England. You seem to me down here to go by contraries. You have an estuary without a river, a Kingsbridge without a bridge, a ducal state kept up without a ducal estate on which to keep it up.'

Beavis did not reply. Crudge turned and looked at him. The moon was full on the young man's face; it was clouded, and his eyes were on the ground.

'You and I belong to the law alike,' said Crudge; 'you are peeling your potato and I am eating at the floury ball, that is the difference. Hope you'll soon get your teeth in.'

'I am in the office of the Duke's lawyer in town; but I am not to continue in a solicitor's office.'

'Why not? The affairs of the family will give you plenty of occupation. Believe me, my boy, there are more pickings to be got out of tottering than standing houses.'

Young Worthivale walked on without answering. He struck a match and lighted a cigar.

'The parrots in Jamaica used to eat nuts,' said Crudge, 'in the days of their ignorance. They have learned to do better for themselves now. They put their claws into the wool of a sheep and swing themselves, bob, bob, bob, against the side of the creature, till with their beaks they get at the fat about the kidney, and they make their repast off that. Better than nuts that, eh? You've your hold on a fat wether; I wish I had your place. All I can say is, bob, bob, bob, till you get at the fat!'

Beavis said nothing, but set his lips tight on his cigar and puffed rapidly.

'I must confess,' said Crudge, 'that what I have seen to-day will remain with me as long as I live. What a remarkable family! The dignity, stateliness, old-worldishness of the lot makes them interesting. They belong to the past. I seem to have come out of Madame Tussaud's, and to have seen wax-work notabilities. I hope you are not offended; I mean no offence. Do you remember the story in the "Arabian Nights" of the man—a Kalendar, I dare say—who got into a palace where everyone was petrified except a prince, who was semi-petrified? I feel like that Kalendar. I am not sure that you are not half-fossilised also. I do not see how anyone can live in this enchanted atmosphere and not be enchanted.'

'I see what you mean,' said young Worthivale. 'You are right, the atmosphere in Court Royal is not that of the nineteenth century, but of the last.'

'There are different atmospheres at different levels,' said Crudge. 'Theirs is too exalted for me. At the top of Mont Blanc men's ears and noses bleed; and I have had great oppression there aloft. I breathe freer now I am down again with you. But you—you belong to the upper crust, after a fashion!'

'Yes,' said Beavis laughing, 'after the fashion of the pigeon in the pie; it has its feet there, but the feet only. I was at table to-day, but not one of the family. My father and sister belong to this exclusive world; they have been like sponges, they have sucked in the surrounding element. They share the views, the prejudices, the delusions of the family and class. To you, what you have seen this day is amusing; to me it is depressing.'

'Exactly so. I am reminded to-day of what is said in Scripture of the world before the Flood. They were eating and drinking, marrying and giving in marriage, until the flood came and swept them all away.'

'You are not far wrong. The flood is surely rising which will sweep them all away. According to popular tradition, the inlet where now the blue waters roll up to Kingsbridge was once a fertile valley, with towns and churches and mansions. The ocean broke in one stormy night and swept them clean away—no, I am wrong—buried them deep, deep in mud. Where was once waving corn is now mud—nothing but mud, and mud that stinks. First the age of gold, then of silver, then of iron, then of clay mingled with iron, and now we are on the threshold of the age of vulgar mud. Sea-wrack for corn, barnacles for men, winkle-shells for palaces !'

' I see you also have a hankering after what is death-doomed !'

' I regret the decay of what is noble and generous ; but it is inevitable. Out of the clay God made men, and out of the coming mud He will mould a new order. When the flat-fish are in the deep sea they have their deep-sea flavour. When they come into our creek their flesh assimilates itself to the flavour of our slime. We shall have to accommodate ourselves to be vulgar, commonplace, to think mud, to taste mud, to have muddy aspirations.'

' I see,' said Crudge impatiently, ' you belong to the upper crust more fully than by the feet. I don't, and I don't want to ! However, the upper crust will have to go under shortly and get sodden in the gravy.'

'Yes,' said Beavis sadly, 'it will go down. Everyone outside can tell the time better than the man in the clock-case. I am in the office of the Duke's lawyer, and am son of his steward; I have plenty of opportunity of noting the tendency of affairs. What, I ask myself, will become of these people, accustomed to the state of a ducal mansion, to the respect and consideration that surrounds them, when cast out, encumbered with a title and a history, reared in one world, hurled into another? To me the scene to-day was one of infinite pathos.'

'The end is not so near as you suppose,' said Crudge.

'It cannot be very distant,' exclaimed Beavis. 'I would give my best heart's blood to save them from ruin, for they are the worthiest people in the world. But I am not blind to their faults. Look there'—he pointed to a row of handsome almshouses in the 'cottage-Gothic' style, each with its pretty garden before it—'Here live superannuated servants of the family rent-free, on pensions. Yonder is the school, entirely supported by his Grace.'

'Almshouses are mischievous institutions; they superinduce a habit of improvidence.'

'That may be true. According to modern

doctrine, charity impoverishes. To give to the poor is to harm them, and should be made penal. The survivals of the old world do not see this.'

'Why should the Duke maintain a school? He should throw the cost on the rates and have a Board.'

'So he should; but he thinks it his duty and privilege to provide the children of all who live on his land with education free of cost, and with religious instruction on the principles of the Established Church. He belongs to a past order of ideas, and that is his view. We who belong to the new order object to gratuitous and to denominational education. The Duke is a patriarch, full of patriarchal notions of obligation to and care for all who belong to him. He would provide for everyone born on his estates if he were able, like the Incas of old Peru.'

'That interferes with individualism,' said Crudge.

'Of course it does; but he belongs to the old school of moral responsibilities. The General, Lord Ronald, belongs to the old school in military ideas; and the Archdeacon, Lord Edward, belongs to the old school in theology.

The Marquess has an honourable soul, but he belongs to the old school of *Laissez faire*. Lady Grace belongs to the old school of sweet womanly culture. Not one of them has any idea how near the edge of the precipice they stand. They look on political dangers as the rocks in their course, and not on financial breakers among which they are running and in which they will go to pieces. It is true that they know they have not the wealth which once belonged to the family ; but they sigh over the past without bestirring themselves for the present. What is to be done for these blind people ? To rob them of their illusion is impossible. It circulates in their blood. To save them in spite of themselves—how is that to be done ? '

The solicitor listened attentively. He said, with a smile, ' Before the Flood they married, and that did not arrest the tide. Before this flood it may do wonders. The Marquess may make a marriage which will save the property.'

' He may do so,' answered Beavis, ' but then he must go about the country heiress-hunting, and this he will not do. He is too proud. Heiresses will not come in troops to be marched past him, as were maidens in the days of

Ahasuerus the king. The Marquess postpones marriage to the Greek Kalends. He reads, smokes, hunts, fishes, yachts, shoots, plants rare pines, believes in his family, and is glued to Court Royal.'

'But has not your father done something to rouse them to a sense of their danger?'

'My father sees with their eyes, hears with their ears, thinks with their brains. To him, the ruin of the Kingsbridge family is impossible ; Providence cannot allow it and reign above the spheres as a moral power.' He turned sharply round to Mr. Crudge, and said, in a voice that trembled with emotion, 'Why are you here? No doubt you have not come here for change of scene, and air, and society?'

'Oh dear no,' answered Mr. Crudge ; 'I cannot afford that. I am here on business—Kingsbridge business. Here we are at my inn. Good-night.'

'May I come in? I will detain you from your bed only a few minutes longer ; but I cannot return till I am satisfied.'

'Satisfied!' echoed Mr. Crudge. 'What satisfaction can I give you? However, come in, and take a glass of something.'

'You must excuse me that,' said Beavis,

entering the coffee-room with the solicitor.
'You understand my position, my relation to
the family. I hope I am committing no indis-
cretion when I ask you for light on your object
in coming here. You say that the end is not
so near at hand as I anticipate. You speak,
then, with some authority. You know the
circumstances. I am warmly attached to the
whole family. I have been reared in the
tradition and reverence for it. My father and
grandfather have been stewards for more years
than I can tell. If the Kingsbridge family goes
to pieces, some of the blame will attach to my
father. Is it not possible that something can
be done to save them? I have no right to
appeal to your sympathy, but I cannot bring
myself to believe that you desire the ruin of
one of the grandest names among the English
aristocracy.'

'I really care little or nothing about them ;
the name of Eveleigh has no more merit with
me that than of Smith,' answered Mr. Crudge.
'But you must not expect of me to confide to
you matters concerning my clients, and to
assist you with advice which may thwart their
interests, which I am here to advance.'

'Of course not.　I merely ask your purpose in coming here,' said Beavis.

'That is no secret,' answered the solicitor. 'Among other debts weighing on the property is a mortgage on the Kingsbridge estate, held by the Stephens Brothers, which has been called in.　The Duke finds a difficulty in raising the money, and he further wishes to raise a trifle of a few thousand.　I have a client who will advance the entire sum.　There is nothing extraordinary in this, nor is the Duke threatened in any way.'

Beavis considered.

'What is the name of your client?'

'Emmanuel.　The transfer of the mortgage will not affect the Duke in the least.　The debt remains, and the interest will be paid to Mr. Emmanuel instead of to Messrs. Stephens.'

'I do not like this,' said Beavis.　'An Emmanuel, I suppose the same man, has the mortgage on the home estate, with park and mansions.　Does this fellow, Emmanuel, know the condition we are in?'

'I know his thoughts as little as yourself,' answered Crudge, who wished to bring this conversation to an end.

'This is the third time the name of

Emmanuel has turned up in the affairs of the
Duke.'

'It is possible.'

'I see,' said Beavis; 'you will say no more.
Well, good-night. At what time will you be
at my father's office to-morrow?'

'At half-past ten or eleven.'

'Say eleven. Allow me time to have an
interview first with the Marquess. Good-night.'

When Beavis was gone, Crudge shrugged
his shoulders. 'No good in that fellow.
Bitten with the aristocratic craze. Wouldn't
I only like to have my claws as firm as himself
in the wool! Bob, bob, bob—till I fed on the
fat of the dying wether.'

On Beavis's return, he saw that there was a
light in the study. His father had not gone to
bed. Beavis was glad of it, as he felt in no
mood for sleep, so he knocked at the door and
went in.

Mr. Worthivale was sitting over the fire,
with a slipperless foot against each jamb of the
mantelpiece, smoking and looking dreamily into
the coals.

'Well, Beavis, seen your friend tucked in
between the sheets?'

'No friend of mine,' answered the son. 'I

never saw him before you introduced him to
Court Royal.'

'Look here,' said Mr. Worthivale, pointing
with the mouthpiece of his pipe at a book that
lay open on the table, page downwards, to
mark the place. 'I've been reading Ouida's
last. What do you think of the story, Beavis?
I rather like it.'

'Never read anything of Ouida's in my
life,' answered the young man. 'Don't care if
I never do. Now I want a word with you on
business, father, if you can spare me ten
minutes.'

'Business!' sighed the steward. 'Eternally
business. After I had done my work for the
day, as I hoped, in dropped that solicitor, Crudge,
to badger me; and now that I thought to
drowse over my pipe and Ouida, in you come,
blowing a blast of business cold in my face to
rouse me. No, I'll talk no business to-night.
Pour yourself out a glass of cold whisky and
water, and smoke a cigar, and then to bed.
You will have to find a tumbler for yourself.
There are plenty in the pantry, with thumb-
marks imprinted on their rims. I told Emily
to put out two whilst you are here, but the girl's
head is like a sieve. She is courting, I pre-

sume. The sugar-bowl is empty; the house-keeper has forgotten to fill that. When I say empty, I am wrong; there is a cake of brown moist sugar at the bottom, solid as pie-crust. The lumps of white had been tumbled in on top—to save trouble, I suppose.'

'I really must have a word on business with you to-night, father. The solicitor from Exeter will be here to-morrow morning.'

'Well, what of that?'

'He will come about the mortgage; and what I want to say concerns the family we alike love, and would save from ruin.'

'Ruin! Fiddlestick's ends!'

'My dear father, the situation is desperate.'

'My dear Beavis,' answered Mr. Worthivale testily, 'I am steward, and I ought to know the state of affairs better than any one else, and I refuse to have it spoken of as desperate.'

'You may refuse, father, to allow their affairs to be called desperate, but desperate they are.'

'You forget yourself, Beavis. You take too much upon you. A raw hand lays on the paint too thick.'

'Their affairs have got into such a condition

that nothing save a miracle can stave off ruin ; and the age of miracles is past.'

'Now, Beavis, you impeach my administration of their property. If they come to ruin, I shall be blamed.'

'Of course you will, father,' said the young man. 'I do not for a moment dispute your devotion to the Duke, your readiness to do all you can to promote his interests ; you have looked at the sun so long, father, that you are dazzled, and cannot see the specks—specks !— the total eclipse that is stealing on.'

Mr. Worthivale was both surprised and offended at his son's plain speaking. He who is dissatisfied with himself is readiest offended. He smoked without speaking, then took a sip at his cold whisky and water.

'Who asked you to interfere ? What right have you to meddle ? ' he asked grumblingly.

'No one has asked me to interfere ; but my love for the family, and the long chain of obligations which binds me to it, forces me to break silence, and bark when burglars menace the house.'

'Menace ! What cock-and-bull story have you got hold of now ?'

'For heaven's sake, father, be serious. I

am down here for a short while, and I cannot in conscience allow matters to proceed without raising my voice to arrest them.'

'Go on!' said his father ill-humouredly. 'Lord bless me. It seems to me that you were in petticoats only a few days ago, and I whipped you over my knee with the back of the hair-brush, and now you are grown so old that you stand up in judgment against your father, and put me on the rack.'

'I entreat you to listen to me,' said the young man. 'No one will free you from blame when the crash comes.'

'What crash?' asked his father doggedly.

'Open your eyes, your ears. I am not steward, but for all that, I can perceive the ripple and the run of the water before Niagara. Consider, what are the estates valued at?'

'That is more than I can say now. With these bad years the land has depreciated one-half. In some places there is no sale at all for it.'

'Guess.'

'Let me see—no, hang it, I can't tell. We only value for succession duty, and, thank God, the Duke is still alive.'

'What are the annual receipts?'

'There I can meet you. In good years forty thousand; now about thirty, perhaps not as much—but this is temporary, temporary depression, only. The seasons have been against us, and American competition. Farmers, again, will not now put up with the outbuildings and the dwelling-houses that contented their fathers. Everything must be new. I assure you we have been forced, literally forced, to spend some thirteen or fourteen thousand on the property of late.'

'What are the debts?'

'You know that the old Duke was an extravagant man. He spent a great deal on the turf—more on the green baize. When the present Duke came of age, he consented to a mortgage on the Loddiswell estate and on the Awton property, to relieve his father from pressing difficulties, to the tune of four hundred thousand pounds. I know we have to pay sixteen thousand per annum on it, which is an awful pull. Then there was the house, which was begun by Duke Frederick Augustus. 'Pon my word, what with building, and new furniture, and ornamental laying out of the grounds, I believe seventy thousand would be under the mark. Then, when the Duke's three sisters were married, they were given fifteen thousand each, which was little enough. That had to be raised by a mortgage on the Kingsbridge manor. The Marquess got among a wild set when he was in the army, and was thrown on the Jews. I wish we could clear off his embarrassments. The sum is not, in itself, much ; say ten thousand, but the interest is extortionate.'

'Stay,' said Beavis; 'the items you have mentioned come to nigh on five hundred thousand.'

' Yes,' said his father, ' you won't be under the mark when you say six hundred thousand. There is the mortgage on Court Royal to Mr. Emmanuel, and there are other matters. You understate at six hundred thousand.'

' Why, that makes an outleak of twenty-four thousand per annum on a nominal income of forty thousand.'

' I dare say. Then the charities of the Duke—subscriptions, pensions, and the like—come to something under twelve hundred. And Lady Grace has her pin-money, and the Marquess his allowance, and both the General and the Archdeacon have something—no, I wrong Lord Edward, he has abandoned his claim.'

'What is the expenditure on the house and grounds, the household expenses, wages, and the like?'

'I cannot tell you, offhand, the items are so many.'

'Now, father, if, as you say, thirty thousand be nearer the present income of the Duke than forty thousand, and twenty-four thousand goes out in mortgages, that leaves but six thousand for everything.'

'These are exceptionally bad times; forty thousand is the true income.'

'The rate at which they are living is beyond even sixteen thousand. You have deducted nothing for all the outs that bleed a property in land. For five or six years the income has not been forty thousand, but there has been no reduction in the style of expenditure. Whence comes the money? Not a burden has been shaken off, fresh are annually heaped on. Let but one of the larger mortgages be called up, and the crisis has arrived.'

His father put his hands to his head. 'You exaggerate. Things are not as bad as you represent them.'

'They are as bad as they well can be. Is there a single estate that is not mortgaged?

There must be a sale of some of the property. On the death of the Duke it will not be possible.'

'Sell!' exclaimed the steward, 'sell the estates! Impossible. Neither the Duke nor the Marquess will consent. One would not dare to make the suggestion to his Grace, it would kill him.'

'If not done voluntarily, it will be done compulsorily.'

'The Marquess will marry an heiress, and clear the property with her money. That is simple enough. How can you be so pig-headed, Beavis? Do you not see that all we want is time? With time everything will come right.'

Beavis sighed.

'What have you to say to this?' asked his father triumphantly. 'Have I the last trump?'

'I have nothing, nothing more to say,' answered the young man; 'I will trouble you no further, father.'

CHAPTER VIII.

THE MARQUESS.

NEXT morning Beavis Worthivale walked to
Court Royal. He had access to the house at
all times. His sister was there permanently,
and he had been about it since he was a boy.

The house was large, forming a quadrangle,
with the state rooms on the garden side. The
Duke had his own suite of apartments; so had
the Marquess, so also Lady Grace, and so also
Lord Ronald. Indeed, the Archdeacon had his
own rooms there kept for him, to which he
could come when he liked, and be at home.
He was a married man without a family, and he
found life dull at his Somersetshire parsonage,
with only three hundred people to instruct in
honour and obedience to the powers that be. He
had an admirable, managing wife, and a safe
curate, very ladylike, absolutely transparent,
whom he could trust to do nothing to surprise or

shock anyone, so perfectly good and colourless was he. The Archdeacon's health suffered in Somersetshire, and he was nowhere so well as at Court Royal, where the sea air and the society and good entertainment agreed with him. Moreover, he was the man whom the whole family consulted in every difficulty, and he was thought and believed himself indispensable to his brothers.

The Marquess had his own valet and groom, and sitting-room, and bed-room, and smoking cabinet. He was a man of considerable taste, and he and his sister had amused themselves in fitting up his apartments in the most perfect modern style. The walls of the sitting-room were gilt, with peacocks' plumes, spread, painted on the gold. The curtains were peacock blue, sprinkled with forget-me-nots.

The carpet was an unfigured olive drugget with blue, green, and gold-coloured mats and rugs cast about it. He had a fancy for old Chelsea figures, and for Plymouth ware, and his cabinets and chimney-piece were crowded with specimens bought at a time when Chelsea was run up by the dealers, and fetched fancy prices. His sister kept his room gay with flowers. That was her special care, and she fulfilled her self-imposed task well. The Marquess always pretended to distinguish between her bouquets and those arranged by other hands during Lady Grace's absence. He told her so privately, that he might not hurt poor Lucy Worthivale, on whom the obligation devolved when her friend was from home.

Lord Saltcombe's cabinet was not invaded or interfered with. There he kept his hunting-whips, his guns, his fishing-rods and the walls were adorned with the heads and brushes of foxes, tiger skins, and antlers of red deer. In one corner was an easel, for he sometimes painted. Against the wall a cottage piano, which he sometimes played. Also a rack of budding-knives and grafting tools, for he sometimes gardened. In the window hung a cage with a canary, which he sometimes fed, sometimes starved, and sometimes overfed. One wall was occupied by his libary, a mixed collection of books: Rabelais, S. Thomas à Kempis, Jean Paul, Spielhagen, Herbert Spencer, 'The Lyra Messianica' and Algernon Swinburne, Victor Hugo, Emile Souvestre, Zola, The Duke of Argyll, Thackeray, 'Explorations of Africa,' and Smith's 'Dictionary of the Bible,' with ' Cometh up as a Flower' and 'Is Life worth Living?' thrust in between the volumes, and a pamphlet on Poultry upon the top of it.

Beavis Worthivale had known the Marquess from childhood, but it cannot be said that he understood him. In fact, no one understood him, yet everyone liked him. He resembled an audience-chamber, accessible to all, containing a closet of which no one possessed the key. He spent his time in reading or in out-door pursuits, yet he had no favourite study and no darling occupation. He was accomplished, knew several languages, was a fair classic, fond of history, and liked books of travel. He read whatever came in his way, changing his style, and subject, and language for the sake of contrast. He skimmed the work he took in hand, but never studied it. Reading with him was a distraction, not a pursuit; a narcotic which enabled him to forget life and its burdens.

The Marquess was already forty, was full of the vigour and beauty of manhood, but it was easy to see that life was to him without object; that he exacted of it little, and cared little for it. Always amiable, cheerful, agreeable, with plenty of conversation and pleasant humour, he

was attractive in society, but was unattracted by
it. He could enter into an argument, but was
indifferent to the side on which he argued. He
argued to kill an hour, not to convince an
opponent. His uncle, the Archdeacon, was
sometimes alarmed about him, lest he should
become a sceptic; but he was deficient in the
earnestness of purpose which would make him
take a line. He accepted traditional creeds,
religious and political, and customs social and
domestic, without consideration, with an under-
current of doubt. He never hurt anyone's
feelings, never transgressed a canon of good
taste. His eyes were open to the errors and
follies of men, and to the virtues of humanity,
but the former roused in him no indignation,
the latter no admiration. Although he was
cheerful in society, this cheerfulness carried with
it an appearance of artificiality, and when he
was alone he lapsed into melancholy or indifference.

He now and then made an excursion to
Brittany or Switzerland; he had even been to
Brazil and South Africa. He came back with
embroidered kerchiefs and carved spoons, lion
skins and stuffed humming birds, and a good
deal to say about what he had seen, but

with no ambition to ascend peaks or explore wildernesses. In politics he took no interest. He rarely visited relatives and acquaintances, disliking the trouble. He professed, and no one doubted his sincerity, that he was happier at home than anywhere else; and more content lounging out a purposeless existence than making an effort to observe and please among strangers and in strange places.

This had not always been the case. He had been in the army, though never on active service. The few years in which he was in the army formed the one epoch in his life in which he had been lost to the sight of his family. The young Marquess, who had been somewhat spoiled at home, with great personal beauty, fascinating manners, a kindly disposition, little knowledge of the world, and a ducal coronet hanging over his head, had suddenly been transferred from the quiet of Court Royal to the vortex of the whirlpool of life. The Duke, owing to his heart disease and advancing years, had been obliged gradually to withdraw from town, and to retire from an active part in the social and political spheres to which he belonged. Lady Grace was always with him; she would not leave her father for long,

consequently the world of Court Royal had
become a very quiet and a very small world.
The temptations to which a young man like the
Marquess would be exposed on entering the
army were hardly realised by his father and by
the Archdeacon.   His sister had not the vaguest
suspicion of them.   'He is a Christian and a
gentleman,' said the Duke, 'and a Christian
and a gentleman, put him where you will, does
nothing unbecoming.'

At Court Royal none knew how he fared,
whether he fought or whether he fell.   His
father heard, indeed, that he was greatly admired
by the ladies and liked by his brother-officers,
and accepted this as his due.   Then the Duke
found that his son was unable to live on the
annual sum allowed him.   He heard that the
Marquess was in debt, and he wrote him a
stately reprimand, but he said to Lord Ronald,
'It is natural.   He must live up to his name
and title.   It is unfortunate that the property
is so burdened and shrunk.'

After that, rumours got abroad that Lord
Saltcombe had been entangled in an intrigue
which was not creditable—with an actress according to one version, with a married woman
according to another.   Nothing very definite

was known, and it was sedulously kept from the ears. of the Duke, Lord Edward, and Lady Grace.

Lord Ronald alone knew the particulars, but he was reserved. He never mentioned the matter to anyone.

Presently the news came that the Marquess was ill at Palermo. 'I did not know that he had gone abroad,' said the Duke. 'Ah! I see there have been signs of activity in Etna; no doubt he went to witness an eruption.'

A few months after, Saltcombe returned home, with the General, who had gone out to him.

Lord Saltcombe was greatly altered, apparently a broken man.

He had been brought to the edge of the grave by typhoid fever, 'owing,' explained the Duke, 'to the absence of sanitary arrangements, which are indeed deficient in the best Continental hotels. I sent out our own medical attendant, otherwise Saltcombe would have been bled to death by those Italian Sangrados.'

Gradually the Marquess recovered from his illness, but though his physical health was restored, his elasticity of spirit, his energy

K 2

- of character, were gone. He remained a prey to apathy, and, as he made no effort to shake this off, habit made it permanent. No one inquired into the truth of the rumours that had circulated, the best-disposed persons rejected them as slanderous gossip.

The Marquess left the army, remained at Court Royal, and settled into the uniform existence of a country gentleman.

When Mr. Worthivale told his son that the marriage of the Marquess was to solve the family difficulties, he expressed his hope and conviction of the entire Kingsbridge family. The Duke was desirous of seeing his son settled before he died, and both the General and the Archdeacon urged him to bestir himself and find a wife. Lady Grace also, in her sweet, fondling manner, approached the subject and endeavoured to arouse him to the duty of marrying. Lord Saltcombe listened with a smile, turned aside the advice of his uncles with a jest, the entreaty of his sister with a compliment and a kiss, and his father's injunction with a promise to lay it to heart. There it ended. He took no step to find a wife, and though Lady Grace invited friends to Court Royal with the hope that one of them might arrest the attention of her brother, the heart of Lord Saltcombe remained invulnerable.

He saw through his sister's schemes and laughed at them. He was warmly attached to her, indeed she was his closest companion. She loved him with equal sincerity and with even greater tenderness. When his foot paced the terraced garden she heard it, came down, linked her hand in his arm, and walked up and down with him as he smoked.

They had plenty to say to each other, but he never allowed her to sound the depths of his soul. The conversation between them concerned the outer life, the events and interests of every day. This association with his sister had a refining and a purifying effect on Lord Saltcombe. She was ignorant of what had occurred during his brief career in the army, and did not inquire. Whatever it was, it had troubled and stained his mind and conscience, and daily intercourse with his sister restored the purity to the mind and the sensitiveness of the conscience, but it did not give him energy and ambition.

Beavis Worthivale was very little younger than the Marquess ; they had known each other from childhood, and had always been on familiar and friendly terms. Beavis, as a boy, had

shared tutors with Lord Saltcombe, and had
been his companion in play. Of late, the friendship had been interrupted; Beavis had been
from home, and Saltcombe in the army. Since
the illness of the Marquess, Beavis had been
unable to recover his place in the intimacy of
the young nobleman that he had occupied as a
boy.

Mr. Worthivale, in his devotion to the
Kingsbridge family, had readily given up his
daughter to be the companion of Lady Grace,
without considering whether it was to his, her,
and his son's advantage. By surrendering Lucy
he had deprived his widowed old age of its
chief comfort, his house of its proper mistress,
and his son of his best companion. Lucy,
moreover, was reared in the lap of luxury,
which she could not expect elsewhere; she was
not likely to marry anyone of rank, and she
was withdrawn from the sphere where she
might have found a husband suitable in birth
and fortune. She would grow up at Court
Royal to be an old maid, a hanger-on of the
ducal house, unable to endure the roughs and
chills of life outside its walls.

In social intercourse men and women act
and react on one another unconsciously. Men's

minds give to those of women the impulse they require, and women's minds afford a corrective and softening influence to those of men. By daily association women are stimulated to mental activity, and men's opinions are rounded and smoothed. From the clash of minds, male and female, the latter take body, the former acquire temper. Woman stimulates man's imagination, man awakes her reason.

Through the Straits of Gibraltar flow two currents—one, setting outward, is warm, and light, and sweet; the other, setting inward, is cold, and heavy, and salt. It is the presence of these opposed currents gliding past each other that saves the Mediterranean from stagnating into a Dead Sea. It is the constant movement of the male and female currents, one giving warmth, the other salt, which preserves civilisation in purity and health. Lucy had suffered by her separation from her brother and father. She had lost mental and moral independence, and Worthivale and his son had lost the comforts of home and the polish which the presence of a lady can alone impart. The steward was unconscious of the sacrifice he had made, but his son saw and regretted it.

As Beavis was walking along the corridor

towards Lord Saltcombe's apartments, the
General's door opened and Lord Ronald appeared in his dressing-gown, a fez on his grey
hair, and a pipe in his hand.

'What, Beavis, you here this morning? No
use going on to Saltcombe ; he is not out of bed.
Here, step into my room and have a chat till
the lazy fellow is ready to receive you.'

CHAPTER IX.

LORD RONALD.

LORD RONALD EVELEIGH, K.C.B., was a widower.
He had lost both his wife and his children. His
wife, a very sweet and beautiful woman, whom
he had tenderly loved, had died of consumption,
after having given him two children, a boy and a
girl. He, as a soldier, had tried to harden his little
ones by exposure, convinced that all delicacy is
due to ' molly-coddling.' The consequence was
that just as he was congratulating himself that
his theory was successful, his children died of
congestion of the lungs. They had inherited
their mother's delicacy, and injudicious treat-
ment precipitated the inevitable end. Left a
widower, and childless, the old General had accepted his brother's invitation, and had settled
for the rest of his days at Court Royal, a spot
dear to him as no other spot on earth, because
associated with his childhood.

He had inherited all the Eveleigh pride of birth, and though he cared nothing for his comfort, and despised luxury, yet he believed the state maintained at Court Royal to be indispensable to the dignity of the family, and respected it accordingly. His own rooms were plainly furnished. Their arrangements were stiff and tasteless. Over the chimney hung his sabre; at the side, on a level with his eye, as he sat in his arm-chair, were three medallion portraits of his wife and his two children.

In manner he somewhat lacked the polish of his brothers and nephew, and in features he was more rugged. His mind was simple and his heart tender. The ambition of his life ended when the earth fell on his boy's coffin, but not its pride: that would remain as long as the family lasted. When Lord Ronald came to settle at Court Royal, he had no idea of the financial conditions of the Duke. There had been hitches in the payment of his annuity, which was charged on the estates; eventually the money had come, though it came irregularly. He recollected the splendour of the house when he was a boy, under the splendid Duke Frederick Augustus, his father—the annual season in town at Kingsbridge House, Piccadilly, the

balls, the round of dinners, the whirl of enter-
tainments, the drawing-rooms, the concerts, the
carriages, the stables, the army of domestics.
Now the Duke never went to town. The doctors
forbade his travelling by rail. Lord Ronald
chafed at this banishment to the country, not
because he liked a season in town, but because
he thought the presence of the family in London
during the season comported with its dignity
and duty to society. The retirement of the
Duke had synchronised with the entry of the
Marquess into the army. A residence in town
was requisite only for Lady Grace, and Lady
Grace least of all desired it. At Court Royal
the customary state was kept up, but then, a
palace on the south coast of Devon, ten miles
from a railway, is not the place where many
people can be found to be impressed by that
state.

After a while his eyes opened to the real
condition of affairs, and he was fain to admit to
himself that it was a happy thing for the family
it had an excuse for not spending the season in
town. The General tried to shut his eyes to
the truth, tried to disbelieve what he could
hardly credit. Without being remarkably sharp-
sighted, Lord Ronald had a sound judgment.

The future began to alarm him. He was much attached to his nephew, but he was angry with him.

'Why the deuce does he not marry an heiress?' he muttered to himself, as he sat smoking, oppressed with low spirits. 'It is high time that the wretched affair which came to an end at Palermo should be forgotten, and the consequences effaced. The creature was not worth fretting over. It was a bad job, but it is done with, and the volume containing that romance should be shut and put away. Is the title to become extinct, the family to die out, because of that piece of damaged goods? What is Saltcombe waiting for? There is nothing to expect. Why is he not man enough to shake himself free of the recollection as he shook himself free of the entanglement? The hope of the family hangs on him. Upon my soul, Saltcombe is enough to drive one mad.'

Heated by his reflections, Lord Ronald had attacked his nephew on the subject more than once, and had been repelled with such coldness that he had retired each time without effecting anything, and thoroughly disconcerted. He lost patience, but did not know what to do. He spoke to the Duke, and his Grace once or twice addressed his son on the advisability of his marrying. But that led to no alteration in his conduct.

Lord Ronald suspected more than he knew. As there was a constantly recurring difficulty about the payment of his annuity, he allowed it to fall into arrears, content if he had enough to defray his ordinary trifling expenses. The Marquess, who was supposed to see to business for his father, apologised to him for the delay, but the General always passed the matter over with a joke about his having no wants in a house where his wishes were forestalled. As his annuity was in arrear he forbore making inquiries, lest he should seem wanting in delicacy. He was told by the steward that the years were bad, the value of land was depreciated, rents were reduced twenty per cent., the farmers could not pay, farms were thrown on hand. He was, moreover, not a man of business, had no idea of balancing accounts, and never could distinguish between creditor and debtor in a ledger. The uneasiness of the steward, his running to and fro to consult with the Marquess, the periodical invocations of the Archdeacon to advise, the troubled face of Lord Saltcombe at times, the difficulty in meeting pressing payments, the

appearance, finally, of that hard, practical-look-
ing lawyer at dinner on the Duke's birthday,
like Banquo's spectre at the table, had made
him very uneasy.

'What the devil keeps Saltcombe from
marrying, and relieving the situation? It is
his duty. Sometimes we go at the enemy in
direct charge, at others sweep round and take
them in rear. We can't dislodge those who
hold the mortgages with the bayonet. Saltcombe must execute a flank movement, with
an heiress. Years slip away, the cloud grows
denser, debts become heavier, creditors more
pressing. Saltcombe is forty, the age is passing
at which he can pick and choose. He will
soon have to take whom he can get.'

The General was thinking this, when he
heard the steps of Beavis, and opened the door.

'Come in, my boy, come in,' he said. 'Saltcombe will not be ready to see you for another
hour. What do you want with him ? '

Beavis hesitated. He did not know what to
say. His heart was full, he could think of
nothing but what troubled him. He considered
a moment, and then resolved to be plain with
the General. It could do no harm, it might do
good.

'I want to see Lord Saltcombe on business.'

'What?—connected with that lawyer fellow here last night?'

'Yes, Lord Ronald. I have no message from him, but I have asked him to postpone meeting my father and the Marquess till I have had an interview with the latter.'

'What is the matter? Is there a secret?'

'No secret—at least, none to be kept from you, my Lord. It concerns the family affairs.'

'Family affairs!' groaned the General; 'then I want to hear nothing about them. I am an old soldier, and not a steward, or a lawyer, or an accountant.'

'For all that,' said the young man, 'I wish greatly to talk the matter over with you. It seems to me that you, Lord Ronald, may do here that which no one else can effect.'

'What is that? I can do nothing. I am the last in the house.'

'You can do much if you will make the attempt, my Lord. Excuse me if I am presumptuous, but I am in earnest.'

'I am sure you are. You are a good boy. Go on. Speak out.'

'It is a very unpleasant thing to speak words that cut the ear they enter; however, in this case it is a duty. I suppose you know that, what with bad years, and the heavy burdens on the property that have been accumulating, and with the inaction of the Marquess, the state of affairs is about as bad as it can be? My dear father will not realise it. His Grace knows, and, I suppose, must know nothing of it. The Marquess is aware, but does not take the initiative, and you, Lord Ronald——'

'I shut my eyes,' interrupted the General. 'No, that is not altogether the case. I see, and am bewildered. I cannot move in the matter. I am awkwardly situated. In fact, the Duke is behindhand with me—not that I want the money, I have my half-pay, but the fact ties my hands, I cannot interfere. I have touched on the subject indeed to the Duke, but he supposes I refer to the losses sustained by the family in my grandfather's time. He was a sad rake. I do not like speaking about it to Saltcombe, for certain reasons of my own. He is reserved with me; he never invites my confidence. So we go on in faith. Times will mend. Something will turn up. Legacies will rain gold. We don't eat our soup as scalding as it is served.'

'Expenses ought to be cut down in every way at once.'

'It has been done. The Duke no longer goes to town for the season. How any further economy is to be practised here I do not see. The house must be kept up, the gardens and grounds maintained in order—the stables— where would you begin? A duke cannot live like a curate in furnished lodgings, on chops alternating with cutlets and steaks, and a maid-of-all-work to cook and dust, and make the beds.'

'Would it not be advisable,' asked Beavis in a low tone, with his eyes on the carpet— 'would it not be well to make an effort, and put up with inconveniences, rather than allow the avalanche to rush down on your heads?'

Lord Ronald took Beavis by the arm, and paced the room with him, before he replied. The old General's face was pale, and his lips quivered.

'My dear boy, you imagine matters worse than they really are. You have allowed your mind to prey on your fears, and they have assumed the appearance and weight of a nightmare. It is impossible for such a catastrophe to overtake us. Think what we are, what our family is, and has been! Think what magnificent estates we have owned—and, indeed, we are not denuded yet.'

Beavis looked up, and saw that the old man was trying to silence his own convictions. Beavis was pained to have made him suffer, but it was necessary for every individual member of the family to be roused to face the danger.

'Dear Lord Ronald, I am not frightened by fancied dangers. The danger is knocking at the door. Would to God it were not so, but I cannot deceive myself. It is. I see you all here lulled in unconsciousness, losing time, letting slip opportunities of recovery which may never return, and delaying retrenchment, whilst retrenchment is availing.'

The General sighed. 'There is a God over all,' he said; 'we must trust to Providence.'

'And do nothing?' asked Beavis.

'What is to be done? I dare not speak to the Duke. Saltcombe would not listen to me, or, if he did listen, would shrug his shoulders and go his way.' After a pause, during which he smoked hard, he asked, 'What was that lawyer lugged in here for yesterday? What has he come to Court Royal about?'

'He has come concerning a transfer of the mortgage held by the Messrs. Stephens to a certain Emmanuel, who has already his hand on the home estate, with park and house, and has negotiated a loan or two besides.'

'What of that?'

'And there is to be another loan of five thousand.'

'That is not much. A trifle.'

'A trifle! but there have been so many of these trifles accumulated, and now they are an intolerable burden. A pound of feathers weighs as much as a pound of lead. Lord Saltcombe should be roused to look into the debts of the family, and form some decision as to what is to be done.'

'You want me to stir him up? I do not relish the task, and I doubt my ability to wake him.'

'He must be shaken out of his apathy.'

'I do not believe it is possible.'

'Then everything remains *in statu quo*— captain, pilot, crew, all must have their sleep out whilst the vessel fills. It is cruel to wake them. They need repose. It is impossible to rouse some, they sleep so sound. All at once the ship gives a lurch, and the waves engulf her, as all wake up and rub their eyes, and ask where they are?'

The General's pipe was out. He turned his

face to the window to hide the emotion painted on it. Beavis had spoken strongly—possibly too strongly ; the words had poured scalding from his heart. He was a young man. He was not called in by the family to consult on its affairs. He had assumed the office unsolicited. Perhaps he was troubling the old man in vain.

The silence remained unbroken for some while.

Lord Ronald struck a match, but could not relight his pipe ; his hand shook, so did the pipe between his lips. He threw the match away, and laid his pipe on the chimney-piece. Then he held out his hand to Beavis, without looking him in the face, and said, 'God bless you, dear boy ! You are acting as your honourable and kind heart prompts. At a time when everyone thinks of self, it is pleasant to meet with one who cares for the fortunes of others.' He sighed. 'You are all of you good, true, all of you—your worthy father, your dear sister, whom we love as our own child, and yourself. You have spoken to me sharply, and I know what it has cost you to do so—you who have been reared in reverence for the family. You have acted as a man of principle should act, but then, what is the good? The transfer will be executed, the fresh loan contracted, in another hour. It is too late to prevent that.'

'Yes,' answered Beavis, 'it is too late to prevent that, but it is not too late to say, " This shall be the last. We have let matters slide their downward way, now we will put on the drag. And the first step towards stopping will be to find out where we stand." '

'You are quite right, but I am no accountant. Your father has the books. Saltcombe is supposed to audit them.'

'Lord Saltcombe must not only look over the accounts, but take an interest in them.'

'Beavis,' said the old General, 'my debt against the estate shall be cancelled; but that is nothing, as it would not be exacted. Let it go. What is this five thousand for? '

'Current household expenses, I presume; but I do not know for certain.'

'Let me find the money. Decline this five thousand. It will be a relief to my mind that I have stopped one additional loan. I have my half-pay, and am able to put aside some money. I have more than I want. If I drop this into the gulf it is only a drop. I know I am robbing my heirs without benefiting the house : but then—the house is my heir. I should leave everything to my dear niece, except a little remembrance to Lucy and yourself. When that hard-faced lawyer comes, tell him the five thousand is not wanted. Damn it, Beavis. I have a mind to throw all my savings into the same hole, but then——'

'No, my Lord, you must not do this. It will only prolong the agony, and rob Lady Grace, as you say, of what in the end she may need. We must get a clear view of the situation before anything further is done.'

A tap sounded at the door, and Lord Saltcombe entered.

'You here, Beavis! Good morning. Uncle Ronald. I heard that Worthivale had been rampaging after me, and suspected you had trapped him. I overslept myself. I sat up very late last night.'

'Doing nothing, I suppose,' said the General dryly.

'Exactly—doing nothing,' answered the Marquess, slightly colouring.

'We have been discussing family affairs,' said Lord Ronald : 'family embarrassments, I had better say.'

' Then I am in the way. I will withdraw.'

' Stay. Saltcombe, we want you to look into matters.'

' My dear uncle, I am at Mr. Worthivale's service every morning, whenever he calls me, to sign leases, audit accounts, and consent to the reduction of rent. I limit him to an hour; I cannot allow more time than that. The office exercises a soporific influence on my brain.'

' You really must be serious. Matters are desperate. Do you know that a lawyer is coming here to-day about a transfer?'

' Well! a transfer is not a nitro-glycerine bomb. I am impatient to make it. I am going to take Grace and Lucy out in the yacht. We must catch the tide. The Sheepwashes are going to meet us at Portsmouth. We are bound for Eddystone.'

' Saltcombe, you do not know how in earnest I am,' said the General; ' I entreat you to stay. I have much to talk to you about, and Beavis here has more.'

Young Worthivale was vexed. The old man wanted tact, and he was doing mischief.

' Beavis is coming with us,' said Lord Saltcombe. ' He wants a whiff of sea-breeze to take the office-dust out of his lungs, and **blow the cobwebs from his brain.**'

Beavis seized the opportunity to turn the conversation. He saw that the General irritated his nephew, without advancing the cause he had at heart. But the old man could not understand his tactics.

'What a man you are, Worthivale!' he said. 'Two minutes ago you were crying, "House on fire!" and now you are agog to be junketing with the girls. I will not be put off like this. You have stirred me up. I will have it out with Saltcombe.'

'My time, then, is yours,' said the Marquess stiffly.

'Very well,' said the General hotly. 'You must marry.'

'Whom?'

Lord Ronald did not answer; the question was not an easy one to answer.

'You remind me of the magistrates of the old German towns, who had the bachelors before them on attaining their majority, and bade them marry within six weeks, or forfeit their rights of citizenship.'

'There was sense in that. You must marry, Saltcombe.'

'Uncle, I will contemplate the five Misses Sheepwash to-day with that view.'

'Do not be absurd. You must marry money.'

'Beavis,' said the Marquess aside, 'you will be at the pier at half-past twelve.'

The General was angered by his nephew's coolness.

'Saltcombe,' he said, 'time enough has elapsed since that Palermo affair——'

'For you to have learned, Uncle Ronald, that I will endure no allusion to it,' said the Marquess gravely, whilst his colour went.

The old man looked him full in the face, and Lord Saltcombe met his eye firmly. He said not another word, but turned with a sigh to the window. The Marquess beckoned to Beavis, and they left the room together.

CHAPTER X.

THE FIFTH OF NOVEMBER.

THE Fifth of November was a great day at the Barbican. *Was*, it no longer *is*. The reason why it is so no longer may be gathered from what follows.

The Barbican offered about the only open space in old Plymouth where a bonfire might blaze, and fireworks explode without certainty of setting the houses round in flames, or of frightening horses and impeding traffic. Moreover, about the Barbican swarm and multiply indefinitely the urchins who most love to celebrate the anniversary of the Gunpowder Plot. They are deterred by no dread of injuring good clothes, are restrained by no respectable parents. They burn Guy Fawkes out of no deep-seated enthusiasm for the Crown and the Bible, but out of pure love of a blaze.

Now, stillness reigns on that momentous

anniversary at the Barbican ; no crackers spurt, no pyre burns, for the police are there in force on the evening to prevent a repetition of such an event as that which took place on the occasion we are about to record.

The broad quay, the proximity of the waters and the coal barges, the good open space before the houses, had impressed the youth for many generations that no place was fitter for the fiery celebration than the Barbican. There were bits of old timber to be had for the asking or for the taking. The owners of the tar and tow and tallow store always contributed a cask, and some black fluid highly combustible. The colliers that lay in Sutton Pool were ready to give baskets of coal.

The adult population of the neighbourhood was in sympathy with the exhibition, turned out to see it, and contributed howls, cheers, and groans.

The Barbicanites had no pronounced political or religious antipathies. It was one to them whose effigy was burnt, they hooted and howled with equal enthusiasm whether the object represented ' Old Boney,' Pius IX., or a Puseyite. All they bargained for was that some one should be burned—who mattered little.

On the last occasion when the Barbican was illuminated by a bonfire, the guy represented a local celebrity. Before that evening closed in, what the guy was to be was known to every in-habitant of the Barbican, except the individual himself. Never had contributions flowed in more copiously, and been given with greater alacrity. Not a householder refused when soli-cited, except only Lazarus, who, when solicited, responded with an oath, a lunge, and a whirl of his stick.

Darkness fell. Joanna put up the shutters as usual, and locked and barred the doors. Lazarus looked with evil eye on the Fifth of November celebrations as a criminal waste of excellent fuel, and he made or pretended busi-ness for the evening which would take him to the other end of the town.

Lazarus had come to entrust the care of the house and the business of the shop very much to Joanna, whilst he carried on business of an analogous but more respectable kind elsewhere. He could place perfect confidence in Joanna. She took as keen a relish as himself in driving a bargain, and in ' doing ' a purchaser. He sus-pected her, indeed, of secreting for her own use some of the money she received, but this was solely because he suspected everybody ; and in this case his suspicions were unjust, for Joanna was scrupulously conscientious in accounting to him for every farthing she spent and received. It was part of her duty to screw down the poor and bleed them of their last drop of blood ; it was part of her duty to throw dust into the eyes of a buyer, and deceive him with lies and disguises ; it was her duty to be true to her master. Joanna was conscientious.

During the day Joanna had observed the growth of a pile of combustible materials before the house, and had engaged in many passages of arms about it. She had remonstrated as to its size and position ; and, finally, she had pillaged it. She had, by watching her opportunities, succeeded in carrying off from it a quarter of a ton of coals which she had stowed in the closet under the staircase, till detected, and then the urchins engaged on the erection of the pyre kept a guard against further pilfering.

When she found that she could no longer plunder the pile, she stormed against the pile-builders, she invoked the aid of a policeman to demolish it. It was in dangerous proximity to the Golden Balls. What if the wind set that way ? When the policeman failed to give her redress, she appealed to the bystanders, the inhabitants of the houses on the quay, but they were all participators in the pyre, had subscribed coin or contributed fuel for its erection.

After she had locked up the house, Joanna retired to a window of the first floor, whence she could follow the proceedings. The Barbican was alive with people, and heads were protruded from all the windows. The evening was fine, no rain fell, no fog hung over the water and wharf. Joanna was girl enough to enjoy a blaze; though old beyond her years in her views of life and of men, she had not lost childlike pleasure in what is beautiful and what is exciting.

Presently Joanna heard the bray of a horn, and the hubbub of voices mingled with jeers, laughter, and whoops. A moment after a crowd of boys, young men, and girls poured down the narrow street that debouches on the quay, carrying in their midst, supported on their shoulders, seated on a chair above their heads, the Guy Fawkes. Torches were borne and waved about the figure, and on its reaching the open space a Bengal light blazed up.

Joanna saw at a glance whom the effigy was designed to represent, and why the celebration had evoked so much interest on this occasion.

The figure was that of Mr. Lazarus. There could be no mistaking it. His peculiarities of costume and attitude had been hit off with real genius. A mask had been made or obtained with a sausage nose, like his, and a smirk on the thick lips, like his. His old fur cap, with flaps to cover the ears, which he wore in the shop, was faithfully reproduced; so also his long-tailed great coat; his black tie, which would turn with the knot under the ear, without a vestige of linen collar. The effigy was represented holding a ham-bone, which it was gnawing.

The crowd flowed from the street, and spread over the Barbican open space. The figure was planted in front of the Golden Balls, and three groans were given for Lazarus the Jew.

Joanna withdrew from the window that the people might not have the satisfaction of seeing that they were observed. Her face flamed with indignation and desire of revenge. She ascended a chest of drawers in the store chamber nearest the face of the house, whence she could watch proceedings unobserved. After the groans for Lazarus, a silence fell on the mob, and expect-

ant looks were cast at his door. They supposed
that the Jew, frenzied with rage, would rush
forth, cudgel in hand, to belabour all whom he
could reach. Disappointed in this anticipation,
they removed the guy to the bonfire, and planted
the figure, in its chair, on the top. Torches were
applied, and amid huzzas and capers, and a ring
of urchins dancing round the pile, the bonfire
burst into lurid blaze.

Joanna saw the faces of the crowd illuminated by the fire. She saw those who lounged
out of their windows looking on, laughing and
applauding. She gnashed her teeth with impo-
tent rage, and clenched her hands. She sat
crouched, frog-like, on the top of a chest of
drawers, with her fists closed, and her chin
resting on them.

'Ah!' she muttered, 'you come to Lazarus,
all of you, when in need; you can't do without
him, and yet this is the reward he gets for help-
ing you in trouble. Never mind, he has you all
in his grip. He will not scruple now to give a
squeeze, and your blood will run between his
fingers. You also! How dare you!' she exclaimed, and pointed to an attic window from
which peered a woman's face. The flames lit
up the room, and cast Joanna's shadow against

the wall, distorting and exaggerating the length of her extended arm. Her finger indicated the woman leaning forth from the garret window, watching what went on below, and enjoying the scene. That woman was the mother of two children. She pawned the blankets every morning that had covered her and her sons by night, for three-halfpence, and redeemed the children's clothes for the day. At night she pawned their rags and released the blankets. Six per cent. is the legal rate of usury, but Lazarus obtained from this widow five hundred per cent. And this woman dared to applaud his being burnt in effigy? Whither is gratitude flown?

Suddenly a report, a roar, then a burst of cheers, followed by a crash, and dead silence!

The ham-bone had gone off! That ham-bone was a rocket disguised in coloured paper. The designer of this exquisite piece of humour had planned that the rocket, on exploding, should shoot out to sea and extinguish itself innocuously in the water; but in the haste and excitement of planting Lazarus on the pyre no thought had been given to the pointing of the head of the ham-bone. The only idea prominent in the minds of the urchins was to set the figure opposite the door of the Golden Balls.

The rocket was from the Government coast-guard stores, liberally contributed by the man invested with charge of them.

When the flame ignited the rocket it went off with a rush and roar in quite the opposite direction to the sea, crashed through a window, and disappeared in the tow, tallow, and tar warehouse.

One precious gift of nature is accorded freely to Englishmen of all ranks and ages—the aptitude of doing the right thing at the right moment ; in a word, presence of mind. Those present, the whole crowd of men and boys— instantly realised the gravity of the situation, and did that which was best to be done—they took to their heels. The first to go was the storekeeper who had contributed the rocket, and he went home as fast as the rocket had gone into the tow and tallow shop, slipped into bed, and called his wife's attention to the clock to enable her to swear that he had been laid up at that time of the evening with a bronchial catarrh. He was followed by everyone who had lent a hand or given a halfpenny towards the celebration. Thus the explosion of the ham-bone cleared the quay in five minutes.

The bargemen looked on from their boats

in complacent expectation of a bonfire bigger than that on which Lazarus was burning. Only a few men stood about the pyre, and endeavoured with rakes to thrust it over the edge of the wharf into the Pool before the police appeared.

Joanna had not observed what had taken place. She had indeed seen the flash of the rocket and heard the cheers, but from her chest of drawers she could not see the tow and tallow store.

Why had the crowd dispersed so suddenly? Why was the bonfire being put out, and the half-consumed Lazarus in his flaming chair toppled into Sutton Pool?

Joanna was roused by the sound of her master's key in the side door. She remembered that she had bolted the door, so she descended to withdraw the bar and admit him. Then her pent-up wrath found vent, and she told him of the outrage.

'Well,' said Lazarus, without signs of discomposure, 'it won't cost me a penny. Have they singed one of my coats? burnt my cap? Not a bit! so it don't matter to me. Run out, Joanna, with your shovel, and see if you cannot rescue some of the coals which are being

M 2

wasted, and then look sharp and get me my supper ready. Dear, dear! The figure was dressed like me, and all the beautiful clothes burning. Don't you think we might fish him out of the water and see what can be done with the garments—they cannot be utterly spoiled! So they are raking out the fire, are they? Scared by the police, I suppose. It is wicked, inconsiderate waste to toss coals and sticks into the Pool. The supper can wait; the apple won't get cold, and it may ripen by delay.'

'What is that?' exclaimed the girl, as a flash of vivid yellow light smote in at the window. 'They're surely never gone and lighted the bonfire again.'

'They are burning what remains of the coal. Oh, the wicked waste!'

'No!' said Joanna excitedly; 'the light strikes from the wrong side of the street.'

She ran to the door, threw it open, and uttered an exclamation of dismay.

The tow and tallow store was in flames; it had burst into blaze at once; all the windows on the second floor were vividly illuminated, and from one a spout of fire issued and ran up the walls. No one lived in the storehouse;

but an old woman, very deaf, occupied an attic, and she was wont to retire early to bed.

A light wind was blowing, likely to carry the flames across the street upon the house of the Jew.

Lazarus stood in the doorway behind the girl. He shared her dismay, but gave louder and more violent expression to it. He swore and stamped.

'The fire will catch me! The fire will burn me and all my pretty, pretty things! Where are the police? Where are the fire-engines? What can I do to save myself?'

'Master,' said Joanna, recovering herself, 'the shutters are up below, so that the basement is safe. There is not much danger to be apprehended till the flames issue from the roof; then it is possible they may be carried our way, or that sparks will be dropped on our roof and make the slates so hot that they will snap and the rafters ignite.'

'Oh, Joanna! run, run with all your legs after the fire-engine!' cried the Jew, wringing his hands. 'If my house catches I am lost— ruined past recovery! I may as well die in it. I could not survive its destruction. I cannot bring my pretty things down; I have no place

where to store them. If they are taken into
the street they will be stolen. There are thousands of beautiful things here no money can
replace. It would take an army of men to
clear them all out in twenty-four hours; and
the wicked flames allow no time. Run, Joanna,
run for the engines! I'll give a sovereign if
they will save my place.'

'Master,' said Joanna, 'lock the door and
admit no one. The fire-engines will be here
before long. Come with me to the roof; we
must protect that. We must carry up carpets,
and spread them over the slates.'

'Carpets!' exclaimed Lazarus. 'They will
be burnt.'

'The carpets rather than the whole house.'

'Not number 247, that is a lovable old
Persian, worth a lot of money, not much worn.
Don't take that.'

'Not if we can do without. We will carry
up the worst, and I will scramble on to the
ridge, and spread the carpets over the roof.
Then you must pass me water, and I will keep
them moist. I'll take a mop, and when sparks
fall I'll mop them out.'

'Oh, Joanna, you are a clever girl! Run!
This is better than the engines; I shan't have

to pay for salvage if they send a little squirt
over me.'

Joanna made no answer, but fetched
buckets. At the top of the house was an
open lead rain-water tank.

'You must help me with the carpets,' said
she hastily. 'Come, this is not the time to
stand bewildered and irresolute.'

The light shone fiercely, brilliantly illumin-
ing the room where they stood, like sunlight.
Everything in it was distinctly visible.

'Not that Brussels!' cried the Jew; 'it is
worth four shillings a yard, and there are a
hundred in it, that makes twenty pounds. I
cannot afford it; I will not throw away such a
lot of money. Here, if it must be, take this old
bedroom Kidderminster, it is full of holes. No,
Joanna, keep your hands off the Axminster, it
is good as new, and has a border round it.'

'Give me the Axminster. I must have it—
it is thick and will keep sopped with water
longest. Help me up with it.'

Joanna went out upon the roof dragging
the heavy carpets after her by means of a rope
which she had looped about them, assisted by
Lazarus from below, who thrust the bundles up
the ladder and through the trap-door. He

assisted, but tempered his assistance with protests and groans. The girl scrambled, cat-like,
up the low-pitched roof, and flung the carpets
across the ridge, or fastened two together, and
spread one on each side upon the slates.

'Give me another,' she shouted. 'Time is
precious; I must, I will, have both the Persian
and the Brussels.'

' The Persian is not to be parted with under
fifteen guineas,' moaned Lazarus, and then half
to himself, ' Guineas are an institution ; say
pounds when a purchaser asks the price, and
when he comes to pay swear to guineas. Will
you have this Kidder. ? '

'It is too thin,' answered the girl. ' See !
The fire is in the upper story, and in ten minutes
will be through the roof. When that gives
way we shall be buried under a rain of fire.
Hark ! '

' You hear the engine coming,' said the Jew,
' and the squealing of the old woman in the
garret. Joanna, take the Persian, take everything, but save my house.'

In a brief time Joanna had covered the
roof on both sides with carpets and rugs of all
sorts and values, and had soused them well with
water. The Jew stood in the tank, up to his

waist, and filled the pails. The girl drew them
up to her by the rope attached to their handles.
She was seated astride on the apex of the
roof, and poured the contents of the pails
over the carpets.

Whilst Joanna and her master were taking
these precautions for the protection of the house
of the Golden Balls, great excitement prevailed
below. The street and the quay were crowded ;
the fire-engine played on the roofs adjoining
the burning house. At a window high up stood
the deaf old housekeeper, wringing her hands
and shrieking for help. The crowd roared,
women sobbed. The ladder was fixed, and a
fireman mounted to the rescue. The mob was
silent ; then cheered as the man put his arm
round the poor creature, and endeavoured to
bring her down. But she was too frightened
by the aspect of the depth she had to descend
to yield, and she struggled, and cried, and escaped back into the room filled with smoke and
twinkling with fire, bewildered, and in her
mazed mind unable to decide whether to risk
a fall or to perish in flames. The struggle was
of engrossing interest to those in the street ;
neither Joanna nor the Jew wasted a thought
on it. They were concerned only with the

precious house of the Golden Balls, and were supremely indifferent to the fate of a stupid old woman of seventy-three.

The firemen and the mob had eyes only for the tow and tallow shop, and the rescue of the housekeeper. When, at length, in spite of her resistance, she was carried down the fire-escape, and received unhurt at the bottom, then only did they observe the proceedings on the roof opposite.

A gush of vivid flame rushed up into the air, over the pawnbroker's house. Joanna saw the peril, and slipped down the opposite incline of roof into the tank. Directly the danger was over, she rose, scrambled again to her perch, drawing a pail of water after her, which she emptied over some fire-flakes that had fallen on the roof. The spectators had held their breath, believing that the flame had swept her away and cast her down, broken and burnt. When she reappeared she was greeted by a cheer, of which she took no notice, not supposing it was given to her.

'There is a hole burnt in the Axminster,' she called to Lazarus.

The Jew, standing in the tank, streaming with water, held up his arm and answered, ' Oh,

Joanna, don't say so! If that occurs again I'll whack you.'

'I cannot help it. I will mend the hole after, if I can.'

' Ah,' said Lazarus, dipping a bucket, ' mend it, mend it! '

In the meantime a consultation had taken place in the street. ' That girl must come off the roof,' said the Captain. ' We must throw our water over it. We can't send the jet till she removes ; it would knock her down. Lord ! she is like a monkey cutting about up there.'

Joanna had seen a spark resting on the roof beyond her reach, and had gone after it with a mop and extinguished it. The firemen knocked at the house-door, but met with no reply. They tried to force it open, but it was so firmly barred that it resisted their efforts.

' Let be ! ' shouted a gentleman in evening dress. ' Captain James, let me run up and dislodge her.'

'If you like, Mr. Cheek. It must be done at once.'

A ladder was applied to the Jew's house, and the gentleman mounted, armed with an axe, broke one of the windows, and swung himself into the house. Joanna and Lazarus, who had

observed nothing that went on below, were
amazed to see him emerge from the attic door
upon the roof.

'Robbers! burglars!' screamed the Jew.
'I'll call the police and have you taken into
custody. I'll shoot you! What is it that you
want here?'

'Come down at once!' shouted the gentleman in evening dress to the girl. 'Come down
from the roof immediately.'

'She is protecting my house from fire!' said
the Jew. 'She shall 'bide where she is.'

'Come down!' called Mr. Cheek, disregarding Lazarus. 'The roof of the house opposite
will give way in a minute, and you will be over-
whelmed with fire. The engine must play upon
this roof.'

'I'll have no squirting here,' said the Jew.
'Joanna and I can manage beautifully.'

'She will be killed if she stays there,' said
the gentleman.

'Not she; she'll slip into the tank and duck,
as before.'

'The engine cannot play till she descends,'
remonstrated Mr. Cheek.

''She shan't stir. You only want an excuse
to make me pay. Mark my protest. Squirt

as you will, you'll pump no money out of my pocket. Joanna and I can manage first-rate without you.'

Without wasting another word on the Jew, Mr. Cheek crept up the slope of the roof, and seated himself on the ridge, astride, opposite Joanna. The girl was wet through and through. Her dark hair was loose, flapping about her neck and shoulders, dank with moisture. The yellow glare of the burning house was on her face, the flames leaping in her dark eyes; she held the mop in one hand, and the empty pail dangled from the other. Opposite her was Mr. Cheek, in fine black cloth evening suit, patent leather boots, white tie, and diamond studs.

'Come down, you wild cat! The roof yonder will be in with a crash directly. Come down at once, and let the engines play over this house.'

'Who are you? Go your way, or I will knock you into the street with my mop.'

'Come down, you fool! do you not realise the danger? You will be burned in a wave of flame in another moment. Down at once, or I give the signal, and a jet of water will knock you over as sure as if you were shot.'

Joanna looked down into the street, and

realised the position. 'I will come,' she said quietly; 'you are right.'

She threw her foot over the ridge, and slipped down. Mr. Cheek followed.

'Oh dear!' exclaimed the Jew. 'Young gent! you've done for your dress suit; but I've some second-hand articles below you shall have cheap.'

'Come out of the tank,' said Mr. Cheek. 'Come under cover at once, before the fire-shower falls. Come in, as you value your life.'

'Mr. Charles Cheek!' exclaimed Lazarus. 'Bless me! I did not recognise you at first. We've done business together already, and, I hope, not for the last time. I beg your pardon, if I addressed you without proper respect.'

'Come in; come in at once. The hose is playing.'

He drew the Jew after him down the step, and fastened the door. Joanna had already descended. They heard the rush of the water above their heads on the slates.

'Upon my word,' said the young man, 'that was a clever idea of yours, covering the roof with wet carpet.'

'My Joanna suggested it,' answered the Jew.

'A girl that, with the head of a man on her shoulders—but eats like rust, and grows like a debt.'

'Well done, you girl!' said the young man. 'I must have a look at you.'

He turned, and saw Joanna, hanging behind, in shadow. He caught her by the shoulders, and drew her to the window, where the glare of the burning warehouse would fall over her face. She was self-composed, and thrust her wet hair back behind her ears, and then, full of confidence, raised her eyes and encountered his.

'Upon my word, a fine girl. Of course there are wits behind such great clever eyes. By Jove! there is devilry there as well.'

He dropped his hands, as with a crash the roof of the house opposite fell, and they seemed to be enwrapped in flame and light as of the sun. Then they heard the rattle of falling ashes on the slates above them, and the redoubled roar of the water extinguishing the fire that had lodged overhead.

None of them spoke for some minutes.

Presently Mr. Cheek said, 'I believe the girl's expedient has saved your house, Mr. Lazarus. I must have a look at her again by

daylight.   Now I am off.   You did not know
me as an amateur fireman, Lazarus, did you?
I am hand-and-glove with Captain James. Often
help.   What is the name of the little devil?
Joanna?   Farewell for the present, Joanna, we
shall see each other again.   Au revoir!'

CHAPTER XI.

WHO WAS RACHEL?

On the morrow of the fire, Lazarus ascended to the roof and wailed over the spoilt carpets. Joanna consoled him as best she could; she pointed out to him the masses of charcoal that had fallen on them, and which, flaming or glowing, would infallibly have split the slates had they fallen on them. 'Then, even if the timbers did not burn, you would have had to call in the masons to mend the roof, and tradesmen, as you well know, are shameless. They would put their nails through the lead gutters to make work for the plumbers, and break additional slates to run up their own bills, and smash windows to force you to call in the glazier, and let the water in on the rafters to rot them, and necessitate the coming of the carpenter.'

'That is true, very true, Joanna; tradesmen

are scoundrels. Nevertheless, I must lament over my loss; it is terrible, it goes to my soul, it corrodes it like canker. The Persian was a real beauty, and the tapestry Brussels was a joy to contemplate. Such colours, such posies of flowers, and no defect anywhere, except an oil-stain in one spot where a lamp had been spilt, and that might have been cleaned for a few shillings. We must have the carpets down as soon as they are dry, and go over them care-fully. With a darning needle and some coloured wools, and little patches put in from old carpets, I dare say you may disguise the worst blemishes. Then, my dear, when you unroll them before purchasers take care to expose the uninjured end. There is a great deal, Joanna, in the roll-ing of fabrics. Always look well which end is most damaged, and begin rolling with that; then, when you show your goods you show to advantage.'

When they redescended to the storerooms, Mr. Lazarus said, 'Dear me! a window broken! That was done last night by Mr. Charles Cheek. He meant well, no doubt, but he has done us a damage that will cost many shillings to repair. Not only are the panes broken, but the wood-work is cut away. He is a gentleman, and when he returns, as he said he would, you had better point out the damage, and make out a case to him that I hold you responsible, and that you will have to repair it from your own pocket. If you manage matters well you may get twice the value of the repairs from him, and I think I can patch up the window myself. I am skilful with my knife, and I have diamonds by the dozen wherewith to cut glass. Putty is easily made with white lead and boiled oil. I don't want any tradesmen in my repository. Light-fingered gents they.' He looked round his storerooms and rubbed his hands. 'What a mighty piece of good luck it was that the tow and tallow shop burnt instead of this emporium of beauty and utility! I am sure, Joanna,' he added, with unction in his tones, 'we ought to be truly thankful for mercies; and I hope, my child, you will take this to heart, and be thankful that the old housekeeper over the way was burnt instead of me and you.'

'She escaped,' said the girl. 'She was saved by the fire-escape.'

'That modifies the case,' observed the Jew. 'Still, though things did not go as far as they might have gone, we shan't do wrong to be thankful. At least, you can.' The Jew looked with complacence at his collections of glass, china, furniture, and clothing, and sighed. ' What a quantity of beautiful things we have here!' he exclaimed. ' I could sit by the hour looking at them, watching the play of light over the cupboards and washhandstands, and in and out among the old clothes. It is lovely. Don't talk to me about landscape! I've seen folks sit on the Hoe and look out over Plymouth Sound, and the Mount Edgcumbe woods, and Maker Point, and say it was all a lovely, ever-varying scene. I can make nothing of it; but I do see a feast of beauty in these storerooms. This is the sort of landscape to gratify the healthy eye. Dear! dear! dear! how could Rachel ever make up her mind to leave this?'

' Rachel!' exclaimed the girl. ' Who was she?'

Lazarus shook his head. ' This is a vale of tears,' he said, ' full of moths. There is one yonder, Joanna; kill it.'

' Who was Rachel?' asked Joanna.

' I wish you would go sharp after that moth,' said the Jew. ' Dear alive! the mischief these moths do is awful.'

' Who was Rachel?' asked Joanna again.

' I will catch no moths till you have satisfied me.'

I will tell you by-and-by.' The Jew sighed. 'Ah! Joanna, I am not the ungrateful old master you may have supposed me. You have done me many a service, but none greater than that of last night. I know I am indebted to you, less the value of the carpets spoilt by the fire. Deduct them from the total and still something remains, not much, but a balance—a small balance. It is pleasant to have a balance in one's favour, is it not, Joanna? I will show you my gratitude. We will have a regular royal debauch for supper. I have some tinned tomatoes. Tomatoes are said to be nutritious, and clear the complexion. I had half a dozen tins and one over from a broken grocer in Courtney Street. We'll debauch on the odd tin. I am double your age, Joanna, and therefore require twice as much nutriment as you, so I shall eat two tomatoes to your one. You, however, may enjoy the gravy. Sop your bread in that, and close your eyes whilst it lies on your tongue. A tin of tomato is sold for one-and-threepence at the grocers and tenpence at the stores. Hang the expense; we will revel in good things for once : and we will wash down the tomatoes with water. That, Joanna, is the drink of the Quality. No more tawny old port, its day is done. Not nutty sherry any more. Not claret, nor Burgundy; not even champagne. They are all played out. Now the Quality are teetotal. Let us be of the Quality also, and teetotal too. Fashions change in drinks as in dress. Now it is cardinal red and marsala, then crushed strawberries and water. Prepare the table, Joanna.'

The girl obeyed without enthusiasm. She placed bread on the table in the kitchen, lighted the fire in the stove to heat some vegetables, and threw a ragged but clean cloth over the table. One candle and the fire in the stove illumined the wretched kitchen.

'I take a little whisky with my water,' said the Jew, pouring some spirits into his glass, 'but I do not approve of alcohol for the young. It stunts their growth, and sows the seeds of a craving for strong liquor which may in after-life bring them to D. T.'

'Who was Rachel?' asked Joanna.

'Upon my word, Joanna! What persistency you have! When you have set your head on doing a thing you do it, and when you have set your head on knowing a thing you give a body no peace till you know it.'

' You promised to tell me.'

' I must keep my promise ; I am a conscientious man, and when I say a word I hold by it. That is the principle of business. Only at the last moment give your word a twist in your direction, if you can. When you have agreed to sell for three sovereigns don't make out the bill for four, but for three guineas.'

' Who was Rachel ? '

' Snuff the candle, Joanna, with your fingers, and—there—don't throw the snuff on the floor lest you set it on fire ; and don't wipe your fingers in your apron where the smut will show, but in your hair, where it will not be seen.'

' Who was Rachel ? '

' I will tell you, child, but really you irritate me with your pertinacity. I will first light a pipe. I don't offer you one, as it is not decent for a woman to smoke. The habit might grow and interfere with your matrimonial prospects. Some women take cigarettes on the grounds that they suffer from asthma or bronchitis. You are sound in throat and lung, Joanna, sound as a bell. Never knew anything the matter with

you except inordinate appetite. Let me have
that chair, Joanna. It is the only one with a seat.
You can accommodate yourself on the fender.'

An old flour-barrel stood in the corner.
Joanna sprang on it and seated herself thereon.
Then, fixing the Jew with her keen eyes, she
asked again, 'Who was Rachel?'

'Really, Joanna,' said the pawnbroker, 'your
ways are inhuman, and give one a cold shiver.
You squat there on the cask like a goblin in an
illustrated fairy-tale. You are not a bit like an
ordinary girl. There is no buoyancy and fresh-
ness in you. Yet—I'll tell you what—I'll do
something splendid to show you my gratitude,
and wipe off my indebtedness. I'll learn you
to dance.

'What!' exclaimed the girl, starting.

'I have a bad debt with a dancing-master,'
said the Jew; 'and the only way in which I
can recover my money is to take it out in lessons. You want refinement and deportment,
and I will do what is magnanimous, and have
you instructed by Mr. Deuxtemps in what becomes a lady. You shall learn to polk and jig
and curtsey like a blue-blooded born mar-
chioness.'

'That's grand,' said Joanna.

'I thought I should please you,' said the Jew; 'I'm not a master to be served without reward. Now I will do something more for you. I will show you the jewels I have, and perhaps let you put some on. I have diamonds, carbuncles, and sapphires fit to make a cat scream. Put out the fire, give me the candle, and follow me to my room.'

He led the way into his private chamber, where was his bed, and where he kept his most precious articles, his money, and his account-books. He set the candle on the table, and unlocked one of the sedan chairs. At the bottom was an iron chest. He opened it and took out some jewel cases. 'No, my daughter,' he said, 'you cannot appreciate the darlings by this light. See this necklace, Joanna, it is made of pearls, and this brooch is of diamonds, so is the circlet for the hair. Get along with you; light another candle, curse the expense! and put the rose silk dress on you. Do up your hair as if for a ball, and I will try the jewels on you. I allow you a quarter of an hour for rigging yourself out. Take whatever you require, but mind and replace all when you have done; also, don't remove the tickets.'

In about twenty minutes Joanna returned.

When she entered she found a brass chandelier hung from the ceiling full of candles and alight, filling the room with unwonted splendour. The Jew sat on his bed rubbing his hands, and when she came in he laughed aloud and clapped his palms on his knees, and kicked his heels against the board at his bedside.

Joanna looked taller in her dress of rose silk. Her neck, bosom, and arms were bare. She had edged the breast and sleeves with rich old lace. Her raven hair was brushed back and rolled over her head, exposing her ears. Thinking her boots too heavy, she had thrown them off, and came in her stocking soles, but as the gown was long her lack of shoes was unperceived. She entered the room of Lazarus without a blush or a smile, perfectly composed in manner, and stood before him under the chandelier.

' Give me the diamonds,' she said.

' No,' he answered, ' you shall have the pearls. An unmarried woman does not wear diamonds. I have a chain of Roman pearls for your hair, and another for your pretty throat.'

Lazarus looked at her with amazed admiration. She was extraordinarily beautiful; her neck long and graceful, her hair rich and lustrous, her features finely cut, and her magnificent eyes full of intelligence. The grub had developed into a gorgeous butterfly.

The Jew contemplated her in silence for some minutes, and then he screamed with laughter.

'Joanna ! your hands, your hands ! '

She put her hands behind her, and coloured. 'I could find no gloves,' she said, looking down.

' A pair of dirty hands is a badge of honour,' said the pawnbroker. 'Don't be ashamed of them.'

' They are not dirty,' answered the girl, sullenly, ' but grimy from work. I have washed and washed, but the black grain will not out.'

'Work, work, work ! ' said the Jew ; ' now dance.'

' I cannot. I do not know how,' answered Joanna. ' Give me the jewels.'

He offered her the cases, and she put the pearls about her throat, then wove a chain in and out among her black hair.

' You are very beautiful,' said the Jew. ' If your hands were gloved you would do famously.'

' For what ? ' asked Joanna.

' For showing off dresses and jewels. When the ladies saw you they'd buy, thinking everything was sure to become them as they suit you.'

Then Joanna said quietly and determinedly,
' Who was Rachel ? '

' Rachel, my dear! Bless me, for the mo·
ment I had forgotten her.   I doubt if even
she was as splendid a beauty as yourself, and
you are handsome enough.   She hadn't your
pertinacity.   How you do fasten on one,
and stick till you have extracted what you
require ! '

' I want to know who Rachel was.'

' There, sit down in the sedan, and I will
tell you.'

' I prefer to stand.'

' Then stand, if you will.   It costs less ; you
are not wearing out the leather of the seat.
Besides, I like to look at you.   I could sell that
rose silk for half as much again if I could show
you in it to a purchaser.   Well, I'm sorry I said
a word about Rachel.   Her name slipped off
my tongue, when my mouth was ajar.   Rachel,
my dear—Rachel was my wife.'

' Your wife !—is she dead ? '

' No, Joanna, I believe not.'

' Where is she ? '

' I do not know.'

' Did she leave you ? '

' She was young, only seventeen, when I
married her—one of my own faith and race,

and beautiful—superbly beautiful. She did not
fancy the business. She did not take to the
house. Her taste lay in stage plays and dances,
and gallivanting. We couldn't agree, and after
we had been married about a year she took
herself off. How ever she could have the heart
to leave all this furniture, and the carpets, and
the second-hand plate, and the red coats, and a
sweet Florentine marqueterie cabinet I then had,
and afterwards sold for twenty-seven guineas, is
amazing.'

' Whither did she go ? '

' I do not know.'

' And you do not know where she is now ? '

' I do not know.'

' Has she ever shown a desire to return
home ? '

' Never, never ! '

' Would you receive her if she did return ? '

' I would not.'

' Why not ? '

The Jew was silent. Joanna looked hard
at him and asked, ' Did she go alone ? '

He sprang from the bed, and paced the
room. His face was changed, and Joanna, who
watched him, was startled and drew back ; the
expression of his features was so threatening and
repulsive.

' I have told you enough,' he said hoarsely.
' I will tell you no more.'

He continued to pace the room. His face
was livid, his eyes glared, his thick coarse lips
were tightly drawn, and his fleshy cheeks were
lined and shrunk.

Presently he turned his head towards her,
but he seemed scarcely to observe her. ' Let
me have him firm here, in the hollow of my
hand,' he said in hard tones vibrating with
passion, ' and I will squeeze and squeeze till
the life is squeezed out of him. Let me grasp
him, and I will tear him down, him and all his
family. I will not spare him, and then I will
caper over him, and you shall dance with
me up and down and in and out over their
broken bones and crushed flesh, and beat out
their brains with our feet, and stamp their marrow into the mire.' Then the door-bell rang.

Lazarus stood still, looking about him con-
fusedly. He put his hand to his brow, to help
his brain to recover its thoughts. Again the
bell rang. Joanna moved to the door to
answer the summons.

' No, no,' said the Jew, ' not in silk attire,
not bedecked with pearls. I will go and see
who rings.'

CHAPTER XII.

CHARLIE CHEEK.

Joanna remained standing under the lustre,
awaiting her master's return. She heard him
in the passage speaking with some one, and
then his feet sounded, shuffling in his slippers
towards the door, followed by a firmer footfall.
Then the door was thrown open, and he
stood back, and bowed, to admit Mr. Charles
Cheek.

'Good heavens!' exclaimed the young man,
'a lady here!'

'Look at her! Look at her well!' exclaimed Lazarus, crowing and rubbing his
hands. 'I'll bet you a foreign coin that you
don't recognise my Joanna.'

Charles Cheek looked at the tall, beautiful
girl with astonishment, and then broke into a
merry laugh.

'Excuse me,' he said, 'but I cannot help

myself. One night we meet on the roof of the house, I in evening dress and you in working clothes; and to-night we meet again, under the roof, I in my morning dress and paletot, and you dressed for a ball, and certain to be its belle. Whither are you going, Miss Joanna, for positively I must go there also, and secure you for half a dozen dances?'

'I am going nowhere,' answered the girl coldly; 'I cannot dance. I am merely dressed, like the block in the milliner's, for the display of the goods.'

'Joanna is going to learn to dance,' said the Jew. 'I intend indulging her in that expensive luxury. She behaved herself, on the whole, well last night, and I must show her my satisfaction. I am a free-handed, liberal-hearted man, as all who have dealings with me can testify.'

'Going to learn to dance, are you?' asked Charles Cheek, looking at the girl with amused curiosity. 'What next—French and the pianoforte?'

Joanna was nettled, and flashed an angry glance at him.

'Now don't she look well?' asked Lazarus. 'Who'd think, seeing her now, that she was drawn out of Laira mud, like a drowned rat, and pawned for ten shillings?'

The girl coloured and her brow darkened.

'Never mind whence she came. I was discovered in a box of preserved figs. She looks as if the rose silk and the pearls belonged to her, and she was born to wear them. Why, if Joanna were to appear at the hunt or the subscription ball, the gentlemen would swarm round her, and the ladies die of envy.'

'She shall go,' laughed the Jew. 'I will send her there.'

Charles Cheek shook his head and laughed.

'Why do you shake your head?' asked Joanna, looking hard at him.

'It wouldn't do,' he answered.

'Why not?' she asked.

'There are reasons that make it impossible.'

'What reasons?'

'There are none,' broke in the Jew. 'If I choose to send her to the subscription ball, who is to say me nay?'

'You could not send her alone. A lady must chaperon her,' explained the young man hesitatingly. He did not wish to hurt Joanna's feelings by entering into particulars.

'Why not?' shouted Lazarus. 'If I will

that she go, I can find plenty of ladies to take her, who *must* take her because I desire it. Ladies of good position will do me a favour if I ask it. They dare not refuse.'

'I do not dispute your power, Father Lazarus; I say the thing is impossible, because Joanna has too much common sense to venture where she does not know her ground.'

Joanna fired to her temples and said nothing more.

The Jew was more obtuse; he said, 'What! don't she look every inch a lady? It is the dress —the dress that makes the lady.'

'Put that rose silk on one of the rowdy women or girls quarrelling or rollicking in the street now, and she will look a bedizened monkey, or something worse. No, Mr. Lazarus; it is not the dress that makes the lady, it is the lady that makes the dress. When are you going to learn dancing, Joanna?'

'I do not know.'

'Where?'

'Here.'

'Who are going to dance with you?'

'No one.'

'Then you will never learn. I will come and be your partner. Lazarus! sweep together some of your Mosaic girls, and I'll bring a friend or two, and we will have the jolliest dancing lessons imaginable.'

The pawnbroker frowned. 'Mr. Cheek, I am not going to turn this house into a casino. I promised Joanna she should learn to dance, and I stick to my word. I can't get my money out of the dancing-master, so I may as well get its worth. That is better than nothing.'

'May I come and help? I am an accomplished dancer.'

'That is as you choose,' answered the Jew; 'only I won't have any of your fast friends here. If you will come in a quiet way, come; only, don't expect to find Joanna dressed up like to-night.'

'Of course she must be in proper attire. No one can dance in working clothes.'

'She has no other.'

'What!—not Sunday clothes?'

'Sunday is nothing to us.'

'What! no go-to-meeting clothes?'

'She never goes to meeting.'

'Nor to church?'

'No.'

'Nor synagogue, nor chapel?'

'No.'

'Good heavens!' exclaimed Charles Cheek, 'what is Sunday instituted for? What are churches and chapels built for, but the display of smart clothes? Lazarus, what a heathen of a Jew you are, not to allow the girl a day on which to shake off her rags and put on fine feathers! Lazarus, we have a little account together; put down the rose silk to it, and let me present it and that necklet of Roman pearls to Miss Joanna. Will you accept the present, my lady Joan, and wear them at our dance rehearsals?'

'I don't know,' answered the girl, looking down.

'Of course she will,' said the Jew, nudging Joanna.

'I said, I did not know.' The girl spoke firmly. 'I will tell you some other time.'

'Will you stop and have a bite of supper?' asked the Jew. 'The festive board is spread. The tin of tomatoes is on the table, so is the bread. True, we have had our light refection, but we will share the remains with you. Water, sparkling and pure off Dartmoor, brought all the way by the great Sir Francis Drake in a conduit. Who'd have thought the great navigator such a fine engineer!'

'Lazarus,' exclaimed the young man, 'I know you can play a fiddle; you tried once to sell me a violin for twice its worth, and played me something on it. Get down an instrument at once, and let me put Joanna into the way of waltzing. She has it in her; a hint, and away she goes. I bet you a sovereign, in a quarter of an hour she will be able to step in a waltz as well as an experienced dancer of seven seasons. Look here, Mr. Lazarus, you whispered the word "supper." I don't like your suggestion of cold tomatoes and cooling draughts. What do you say to pigeon or beefsteak pie and a bottle of champagne?'

The Jew's eyes twinkled. 'Very well,' said he, 'so let it be. I'll run down the street and get what you desire—I cannot send Joanna in her present costume—and be back in three seconds. Then I'll give you a scrape on my fiddle—Strauss or Waldteufel—and do what you can with Joanna. I know her. She don't want twice telling to learn a thing, not she. Of course you pay for the pie and the champagne. I am not responsible.'

'Certainly. Tell me what I have to pay, and I will refund the outlay.'

'Would you mind advancing half a sovereign ? ' said Lazarus. ' I have only three half-pence in my purse.'

Mr. Cheek tossed him the money. Lazarus caught it as sharply as a dog snaps at a bit of meat. When Lazarus had disappeared, Joanna looked steadily at the young man, and asked, ' Why is it impossible for me to go to a ball ? '

' I did not say that you could not go to a ball.'

' No, you implied that I had too much sense to appear in the society of gentlemen and ladies.'

Charles Cheek slightly coloured, stammered, and said, ' Well, I did mean that.'

' Why ? '

' You ask me ? Do you not yourself under-stand ? '

' No.'

He thought for a moment, and then he said, ' My girl, you would not think of going to a grand ball, as I saw you last night, astride on a gable, a pail in one hand and a mop in the other, clothes and hair streaming with water, and a black smirch of soot across your fore-head—with, moreover, a smock in holes, and one slipper on, the other off.'

' No, I would not.'

'Very well. You would appear as you are now?'

'Yes.'

'But more dress than this is expected. Your mind must be in rose silk and pearls. Your tongue must be in full dress; your manner must be the same. Let me tell you that, among ladies, their tongues and their minds are never with one slipper off, the other on, never with sooty smears across them, but always wreathed with pearls and rustling in rose silk. They have never known anything else. Do you understand me?'

Joanna put her finger to her lips and considered. As she thought, she put forward one of her feet; Charles Cheek noticed it at once. 'Joanna,' he said, 'you are dressed like a princess, but you betray yourself by your stocking. You are not only shoeless, but you have a hole in your sock.'

The girl started, and drew back her foot.

'I do not want to hurt you,' he said good-naturedly; 'I use this only as an illustration of what I mean. If you were in the society of gentlemen and ladies, you would betray yourself by your stocking holes.'

'I would not wear——' She stopped.

'No. I do not mean stockings. I mean the gaps and shortcomings in speech and culture.'

She looked intently at him for a minute.

'I have never seen real ladies and gentlemen—never, that is, except on business. Are you a real, proper gentleman?'

Charles laughed. 'That is a cruel question, Joanna; I cannot answer it. You must inquire of others.'

Joanna considered again. Presently she said, 'Here I see nothing but raggedness, wretchedness, and care. I know nothing of a richly clothed, happy, and careless world. Here I am surrounded by poverty, and the air is charged with the dust of old clothes and the reek of Laira mud; the light that comes through these windows is never clean; the air is always stale. Why should not I sometimes spring up into the region of light and liveliness? Lazarus often tells me I am a maggot, but a maggot becomes a moth with wings of silver. Am I to be always a grub—never to rise? If Lazarus offers me the chance to have a short flutter, may I not accept it?'

'You are a queer girl,' answered the young man. 'Take care not to leave your proper element. Have you ever heard of the flying fish ? The fish have fins so long that they can rise on them a little way out of the waves, and the silly creatures think they are birds ; so they spring above the water, and are immediately snapped up by gulls.'

Joanna laughed. ' I am not afraid of that ; I am more likely to snap the gulls than the gulls snap me.'

' You are a comical girl,' said Charles. ' It is a pleasure to hear you talk. Are you happy in this den ? '

' How can I be ? Look about at the den. I will show you where I sleep, on a sack full of shavings under the counter. My food consists of crumbs of bread, rinds of cheese, and apple parings, which Lazarus cannot eat. My play-ground is a backyard in which the only green thing is the slime on the pavement. Lazarus has no Sundays and I no Sabbaths, so I never have a holiday.'

' Then why do you not leave ? '

' Because I cannot. I am pawned.'

' Pawned ! '

' Pawned by my mother. I cannot leave. She expects me to remain till she redeems me. There is no help for it. I must abide where I am till she returns.'

'Where is your mother?'

'I do not know.'

'Good heavens! and you are enslaved all this while, without power of obtaining your freedom!—Till when?'

'Till I am nineteen years old—that is, seven years since my mother pawned me. If she does not bring the ticket and release me before then——' She did not finish the sentence.

'Well then——?'

'I will kill myself.'

'Nonsense, Joanna. You are a little goose. I can't follow your scruples. I see no right and wrong in the matter—no such obligations as you fancy.'

'I do not suppose you can. You belong to the gentry.'

'Well!' Charles Cheek laughed. 'Have gentlefolks no consciences?'

'No, none at all,' she replied.

'How do you know that?'

'Because I know them through Lazarus' books and the society papers.'

'And you have no other sources of information?'

'I want no other. Lazarus deals with gentlefolks of all kinds, and through his account books and what he tells me I know about most of the officers and officers' wives and gentlefolks of every sort here, and the society papers tell us what the rest are like in London.'

'Every picture has two sides, Joanna. You see only the back.'

'Has society another side?'

'Of course it has.'

'I cannot believe it. The world of men is cut into two halves—the rich and happy and vicious, and the poor and miserable and deserving. I will not say that the poor are good—I see too much of them to assert that, but they deserve what is better than they have. They cannot be good because they are wretched. No one can be good under a hundred and fifty per annum.'

Mr. Cheek laughed. 'Or with an income above that limit.'

'Below that sum come gnawing care, and grasping for coin, and biting and eating one another. Above that sum, idleness and waste and luxury.'

'And so, you comical socialist, you take as gospel all you read in the society papers, and believe in the utter corruption of the aristocracy?'

'It is in print. What I read is read by

tens of thousands. The old woman who sells shrimps and ginger-beer, the barge-man in the coal-boat, the men in Eddystone, the board-school children, all read the society papers, and gather from them convictions that the upper ranks of life are corrupt to the core, and burn with desire to tear them down in the interests of morality, and cast them in the gutter. Why should we lie on sacks of shavings and eat cheese rinds, and never leave the Barbican and escape the smell of Sutton Pool, and they bed in down and fare sumptuously, and go to opera and ball in the season and to their parks or to the sea out of season? I would I had the re-making of the world. I would cut the rich down to a hundred and fifty, and pull up the poor to the same figure. Then we should have an equalisation of happiness. Hark! here comes Lazarus ; I hear his key.'

'Joanna, it is rare fun to hear you talk! Tell me, will you accept my present of the dress and chain ? '

'I will,' she answered. 'I would not at first, because I doubted whether you laughed at me or pitied me.'

'I certainly pity you.'

'Then I take your present, and thank you.'

The Jew entered, a basket on one arm, a bottle under the other. He was elated and chuckling.

'I have been absent some time,' he said ; 'I found the wine merchants closed, and I would not have bad gooseberry at the tavern. Here is the pie '—he opened the basket—' and a dozen raspberry tartlets, and a pound of clotted cream. I understood you to say tartlets, Mr. Cheek.'

' As you will.'

' I am positive you desired me to buy them ; I particularly remember that you specified raspberry. Also cream at one-and-four. The pot I can return, so it will not be charged. I had to carry the cream very tenderly, so as not to spill a drop. Then,' he added, ' I have added my own contributions to the feast, one apiece. " Blow the expense ! " said I, " oranges are now at a price within the reach of the poor— twenty-one for a shilling." '

' You will produce your violin ? '

' Certainly. I hope Joanna has entertained you whilst I have been away.'

' Famously. She is a comical girl, and I enjoy a talk with her—the first of many, I trust.'

CHAPTER XIII.

THE EMS WATER.

JOANNA was unable to sleep that night. The champagne had excited her brain, and she lay watchful under the counter in the shop, tossing on the sack of shavings. The night was cold, so she had thrown a military greatcoat over her, and a black rug across her feet. She mused on what had taken place—the wonder in the eyes of the young man when he saw her in the silk attire, the interest she had awakened in him by her conversation and her good looks. She had a cool head, and was able to weigh the value of his admiration. She had measured the man. She knew him to be amiable, with fair abilities, but shallow. He was good-natured and weak. He had promised to return, but she placed no reliance on his promises. If he had nothing better to amuse him, he would come, not otherwise. But though she was aware that his liking for her was not deep, easy to be effaced, she was pleased with having aroused a transient fancy. A light had flashed into her dull life. She was unaccustomed to amusement of any sort. She had not associated with the children of the Barbican, nor shared in their games. Her master's unpopularity had affected her; the exigencies of his service had cut her off from social pleasures.

She had spoken to Mr. Cheek with force and freedom on the distinction between the lots of rich and poor. She had spoken more strongly than she felt. Her ideas formulated on her tongue as she spoke. She had no sympathy with the poor; they were the proper prey of a usurer. That they brought wretchedness on themselves by their own recklessness, improvidence, and idleness, she knew very well. She took advantage of their necessities without compunction. But she felt keenly her own condition and her powerlessness to escape from it. The enigmas of life, that lie unperceived in savagedom, rise into prominence with civilisation, and as culture advances become more perplexing and insoluble.

Joanna sat up under the counter. Lazarus was asleep. She could hear his snoring. He

was a noisy sleeper, and though his door was
shut and locked, his nasal trumpetings were
audible in the shop, and annoyed the girl.
On the counter above her was a tin case containing a ball of twine ; the end of the twine
hung down over the edge, and as she tossed on
her sack touched and tickled her face. She
laid hold of the end of string and threw it up,
but it fell back on her face. Then she began
to pull at it, and unwind the ball, and rewind
it on her fingers. The ball seemed interminable.
She was engaged on it half an hour, running the
twine out and rolling it again. She did it for a
distraction, and as she did it the thought came
on her that it was thus with her life ; she was
drawing out yard after yard of existence, all
alike, with a knot here and there, all much the
same, and then, suddenly—there was an end.
It mattered nothing when the end came, the
entire string was so utterly uninteresting.

As sleep would not come to her, she shook
off the rug and crawled from her bed. The
night was cold, and she was partially undressed.
Therefore she drew on the military greatcoat.
Thus attired, in her stocking soles, she stole out
of the shop to the stairs. She had a favourite
retreat on the roof, where she could be quiet

and think. There she had a few pots of flowers and a little stool. Perhaps the night air would bring drowsiness to her lids. A problem was perplexing her restless mind; she could not sleep with that unsolved. The problem was this: Why were artisans and domestic servants dissatisfied, and why were shopkeepers content with their lot? All were workers alike. Lazarus worked harder than most day labourers; the man at the ham and pork shop worked like a slave, so did the greengrocer, so did the paperhanger next door but one. These were cheery folk, and did not grumble at their condition. It was otherwise with the journeyman plumber, and carpenter, and the factory hand, and the maid-of-all work. These were impatient of their position and hated their labour.

Joanna traversed the storerooms. The gas-lamp in the street threw in sufficient light for her to see the furniture, and to thread her way without touching and upsetting anything. [Had the lamp indeed been extinguished she would have found her way noiselessly about those rooms, and brought from them whatever was required. She went to the window, and looked across the way at the ruin of the house that had been consumed the night before. Every pane of glass was broken ; the entire roof had fallen in. Then Joanna went into the room from which the carpets had been removed to protect the roof, and which still covered it. Here alone was an empty space. Joanna cast off the thick coat, and sprang lightly into the middle, stood on tiptoe and threw about her arms and twirled as she had seen in pictures of ballet-dancers. Then she hummed to herself a waltz of Strauss, and began to dance, with fantastic gesture, the step she had acquired that evening from Charles Cheek.

Presently, fearing lest her tread should disturb the Jew, she reinvested herself in the long grey overcoat, and ascended the ladder to the roof.

The cold air made her shiver, but it was fresh after the close, dust-laden atmosphere of the house. The stars were burning brightly overhead.

She looked at her plants ; several of the pots were knocked down. One was broken, and the earth had fallen from the roots. She had the ball of twine in the pocket of the coat, and she took from it sufficient to bind together the broken sherds. She cut the string with her teeth; then she put in the earth again. The geranium in the spoutless teapot must come in, and sleep for the winter. The fuchsia must have fresh earth about the roots; the Guernsey lily needed to be divided. All this would have to be done by daylight on the morrow. Then she took up a pot in which was heather, a little heather in peat she had taken up wild and carried home on one rare occasion when she had been in the country for a holiday, on Roborough Down. She loved the heather above every flower she had, yet it was sickly in confinement. Perhaps it was cold up there on the slates. So she took the pot in her arms, seated herself, hugging it, with the greatcoat wrapped round her and the heather, and began to think. She could not see into the streets from where she sat, as the parapet cut them off, but she saw the yellow haze that hung over Plymouth, the reflection of the lights in the fine vapour that overarched it. The taverns were shut; no drunken men were about the Barbican. The outline of the citadel stood dark above the harbour. She could see the lighthouse at the pier-head, and far out, reflected in the quivering water, the spark of Mount Batten light. Joanna thought first of her flowers, and then, last of all, of the problem she had climbed to the roof to solve: Why did the labouring class hate work, and the trading class love it greedily? The girls from the country streamed into Plymouth, because they had been taught to read and write —to read novels and write love-letters—and therefore counted themselves superior to feeding pigs and making butter. They went into service, and when they found that there they were expected to dust chairs and wash up breakfast things they went on the streets. That was an everyday story. They fled work because work was hateful. The young men poured into town from the country to escape the plough and the spade, and when they found that they were expected to work at a trade, they earned their bread with resentment at their hearts, because *prava necessitas* insisted on labour; and they blasphemed God and dreamed of upsetting the social order because forced to work. Why was this? The moment, however, that the parlour-maid became a married woman and had a home to care for, she toiled without grudging time or labour. The moment the artisan opened a shop and worked for himself, he was reconciled with Providence and the social system. Why was this? Unconsciously,

Joanna had struck the solution. Content came when man and woman worked for self. Discontent was consequent on working for others. 'This is it,' she exclaimed; 'to be happy and good one must care only for self, and not a brass farthing for anyone besides.' That was Joanna's philosophy of life, hammered out of her experience and observation.

Having arrived at this conclusion she stood up. 'I am cold,' she said, 'so is the pot of heath. We must go in.' Then she stole downstairs.

Joanna descended very softly, lest she should rouse Lazarus. She listened on the stair for his snore. If that were inaudible, it would behove her to walk warily. He might be lurking in a corner or behind a door, ready to leap forth with his stick and batter her. No—she did not hear it. She put foot after foot before her most cautiously, listening and peering about her in the dark. Then—she heard a sound, an unusual sound, which made her heart stand still; she stood with poised foot and uplifted hand to her ear.

The sound came from the back kitchen, and simultaneously she heard the choking snort of Mr. Lazarus in his bedroom.

She crept so noiselessly down the last steps
that she would not have scared a mouse, and
craned her neck to see who or what was in the
back kitchen. In that back kitchen was a low,
square window over the sink. Her eyes were
sufficiently accustomed to the dark for her to
see that the window was obscured by a dark
body. She made out that the sash had been
thrown up, and that a man was crawling in at
the narrow opening. She saw also, by a feeble
glimmer, that a second man stood in the outer
kitchen, holding a dark lantern, waiting for his
fellow to enter as he had come in.

Joanna did not scream. Her lungs were
more powerful than when, as a child, her
mother had commended her powers of screaming. She knew that if she set up an alarm the
first impulse of the burglar would be to stop
her voice, and that he would have no scruples
as to the manner in which he attained his object.
Joanna had matches within reach, but she did
not strike a light. She was too wise to expose
herself to observation. She preferred observing
unseen. She considered what she had better
do, and, having rapidly determined, proceeded
to take her course with celerity, circumspection,
and silence. She stepped, unobserved, from

the stair into the passage leading to the chamber of her master and to the shop. She was sure that the burglars would not ascend to the store-rooms, to burden themselves with sets of bedroom crockery or chests of drawers. They would look for what was most valuable in the smallest portable form, money and jewels and plate ; and all these were in the bedroom of Lazarus. This was the point of attack that must be defended.

Now the thought crossed the mind of Joanna that she might slip into the shop, close the door between and open the shop door, run into the street and give the alarm ; but her blood was up. She was a brave girl, she was also a girl quickly roused to anger, and she was now, not afraid, but furious. If men had dared to break into her master's house, she was determined they should not leave it without a lasting lesson not to do so again, at least while she was there to protect it.

Joanna was unprovided with firearms. Lazarus had a revolver in his room, always loaded ; but he took time to rouse, being a heavy sleeper. Against the wall ranged in the passage were the bottles of Ems water. Above, on nails, hung a large locked saw. She took it down, and removed the wooden cover to the teeth. Then she crouched on the ground, waiting, watching, like a terrier at a rat-hole. Her eyes were on the back kitchen door.

Presently she saw the faint light of the closed lantern in the front kitchen, and heard the fall of bare feet on the floor. She raised her arm with deliberation, with eyes riveted on her object, and flung a bottle of Ems water, not under hand, as a girl casts, but as a boy hurls. A gasp, a crash, and a smothered cry! The lantern fell on the kitchen floor. At once Joanna glided forward, secured the lantern, and retired whence she had crept, and covered the light with her coat. The kitchen was dark as pitch. She heard a spluttering and grumbling, then a whispered query from the second burglar —what was the matter? where was the light? Suddenly she sent a ray across the space; it fell on a face with staring eyes, a coarse ragged beard, and a great cut across the brow from which blood was running. That was all. With a click the lantern was closed, the light cut off, and with level directness another bottle struck the same mark.

Then came a scuffle, a cry, and curses. She

listened, holding the light under the flap of her greatcoat, and did not stir till she was sure that the burglars, hurt, frightened, bewildered, were scrambling back through the outer kitchen, one falling over or clinging to the other. Then, once again, she sent a beam of light upon them. She let it travel from one to the other. She marked both faces. One man had his hand to his head, and hand and face were smeared with blood. Again she flung a bottle, and the man went down. Then she retired to the shop and put on her shoes. She drew on her shoes because the floor of the kitchen was strewn with broken bottles, and she did not choose to cut her feet. Then she took the saw and pursued the burglars. One was already through the window over the sink, the other was making his way through. With that generosity which is found even among criminals, the uninjured burglar had helped his wounded companion through before he attempted escape himself. Joanna attacked this man with the saw.

Hitherto the only sounds to which they had given vent were muffled cries and groans. Now this second burglar uttered screams terrible to hear.

Presently Lazarus appeared in his nightgown, holding a candle, white with fear, with a pistol in his trembling hand.

'Put down the revolver,' called Joanna. 'I've done the job without you.'

'What is the matter? What is it? Joanna! O Lord! O Lord! Whose are these horrible shrieks?'

'He is like to shriek,' said the girl, wiping her brow with the left hand; 'you'd shriek, I reckon, if sawed at whilst crawling through a little window.'

'What are you doing?' asked the bewildered, frightened Jew.

'Sawing, I tell you,' answered the girl. 'Don't come forward; you'll cut your feet on the broken bottles. There! we are clear of them.'

'Clear of what?'

Joanna quietly shut the sash of the window over the sink.

'I see how it was done,' she said; 'they removed a pane, and so got their hands in to turn the hasp.'

'Who, child, who?'

'Burglars, of course. Who else?'

'Burglars in my house?'

'They won't come again,' said the girl dryly.

'Stay where you are, and let them get away through the back-yard door. They came over the wall, but neither of them is in a fit condition for scrambling now.'

'But, Joanna!'

'When my mother pawned me,' said the girl, 'she said I could scream enough to scare away robbers. I'm older now. I make the robbers scream.'

So Joanna was false to her philosophy ten minutes after having formulated her view of life.

CHAPTER XIV.

THE MONOKERATIC PRINCIPLE.

'You are a capital girl,' said Lazarus, 'and I will not forget what you have done. The Ems water was no loss to cry over, as the demand for it is slack. I am grateful, and to show you my gratitude I will give sound advice.'

'Advice!' echoed Joanna contemptuously.

'That costs nothing. Take mine, and get into your clothes.'

'To be sure I will,' said the Jew. 'Whilst I am getting on my garments, do you, Joanna, see that the back-yard is clear, and bolt and bar the door. I'll provide that the sink window is fastened up to-morrow. Every down-stair window but that has iron bars. That, I suppose, was neglected because it looked into the yard. How did they get the window open?'

'Go to your room and get on your clothes, and I'll find out.'

'To be sure. I am shivery, and might catch cold, and be forced to send for a doctor. Look here, Joanna; after this affair there will be no more sleep to-night for either of us, so I will allow you to light the fire. We will sit up and talk matters over till daybreak.' Then he retired to his room, taking the candle with him, and locking his door behind him.

Joanna took the lantern. She examined the window that had been entered. The burglars had affixed a diachylum heart-plaster to a pane of glass, and cut the pane out. By this means it had been removed noiselessly, and was laid outside against the wall, unbroken. She found the door in the yard open, as she expected. The burglars had come in over the wall, but had escaped by means of the door.

She made all the doors fast, and put a tray before the paneless window to exclude the cold. Then she lighted a cheerful fire in the stove. By this time Lazarus was clothed and came out of his room.

'I think,' said he, ' as there is a good fire, we might get the Persian carpet down from the roof and dry it. Always kill two birds with one stone, if they will stand for it.'

Assisted by the Jew, the carpet was brought down and hung on a horse in the kitchen.

Then Lazarus drew his chair to the fire and warmed his palms at the blaze.

'When I consider,' said he, ' the deliberation and coolness with which you worked off those burglars, all I can say is you ought to have been a Jew.'

The girl made no reply. It was a matter of indifference to her whether she were a Jew or a Gentile. She collected the broken stone bottle sherds from the floor and mopped up the slop of mineral water.

'I have been counting the Ems water,' said Lazarus; 'there are but six bottles left.'

'You are not going to make me drink the remainder, are you,' asked Joanna, standing up, ' to show that you are grateful because I saved your house from being burnt and your throat from being cut?'

'No, I am not,' answered Lazarus.

'Whatever you do won't cost you much,' said Joanna.

'Now, don't say that,' Lazarus remonstrated, nettled with the truth of the observation; 'I am not bound to do anything for you.'

'Nor was I bound to save your roof from flames and your throat from the knife.'

'How coarsely you speak!' said Lazarus. Then he was silent, looking into the fire and then at Joanna, with something trembling on his tongue, yet doubtful whether to utter it. Probably he had resolved not to speak, for he merely said to himself, 'Ems ain't bad; but its day is over. Double dahlias one day, single next. Such is the world. So the pendulum swings.'

Joanna continued her work without a reply.

'You are a good girl,' he added, looking into the fire; 'there is a splendid future in store for you, only you don't know it. When that does break on you you will cry out, "O Lazarus! O Lazarus!" and swoon away for delight.'

'I'd rather have something now,' said Joanna; 'the gift of a sheet in winter is better than the promise of a blanket in summer.'

'You are fed, clothed, shod at my expense,' said the Jew. 'Your mind has been formed and your morals moulded by me. You have no cause to grumble.'

'Fed on scraps, clothed in rags, and educated to keep your accounts,' muttered the girl.

'You are discontented, peevish, and don't know when you are well off.'

'Every man knows the warmth of his own jacket,' said Joanna.

'How I've stored your mind with knowledge!' exclaimed the Jew. 'You know the value of an article as well as I, whether furniture, plate, clothing, china. I've taught you a lot of useful information, summing, bookkeeping.'

'What is the good of striking matches for those who don't want light?' asked the girl sullenly.

'What has put you out of temper to-night, Joanna?'

'I have good reason to be in bad humour. What have I done for Mr. Cheek that he should give me the silk dress and the necklace? Nothing but amuse him for an hour. What have I done for you? Everything. I have saved your house from fire and your throat from the razor. What do I get in return? Nothing.'

'I am not ungrateful,' said Lazarus, seriously. 'Wait a bit longer, my girl, and I will show you that I am not. I cannot tell you

now what I will do for you, but I will in time.
I promise you this—you shall have a reward
such as you have not dreamed to possess. Have
I ever failed to keep my word, Joanna? No,
never; it don't pay in business to be shifty
about promises. Now you have alluded to
Mr. Charles Cheek, I wish to speak to you
about him, and to give you a word of advice.'

'Which again will cost you nothing,' threw
in the girl.

'It is clear to me, Joanna, that Mr. Charles
Cheek is interested in you. Now, you are no
longer a child. You have swelled on my good
fare into a big, handsome girl, not at all of the
ordinary type. If Mr. Cheek continues to come
here, you are the attraction. I am well pleased
that he should come here, and provide beefsteak pie and champagne, and if you behave
discreetly all is well. He is weak and careless,
and you may entangle him in a web whilst I
suck his blood ; but let it be understood between us that I will not have you entangled
in any thread of his spinning—not caught by
finger or toe, Joanna. Keep your head clear
and your heart cool. Be very careful of yourself, not to allow the smallest feeling of regard

to lodge in your bosom ; if you do you lose all control over yourself.'

' What is the advantage of offering a wig to one with a head of hair ? ' asked the girl contemptuously. 'I know how to take care of myself. Tell me now, who is this Charles Cheek ? '

' He is the offspring of the Monokeratic principle.'

' Of what ? '

' Of the Monokeratic system of business,' answered Lazarus.

' I do not understand.'

' I will explain to you. Sit down, child, on the other side of the fire. Old Joe Cheek— Lord ! I knew him well, years ago, with a little shop and a long head. He was in Devonport when he began, but Devonport wasn't a sphere for one like him, so he moved up country. Not content with a small retail shop, he opened a store of combined grocery, haberdashery, stationery, hosiery, wines, drugs, and oriental goods, and sold everything for ready money. Others have done the same, but not on the Monokeratic system.'

' What is that ? '

' Well, he advertised all over England,

" Try Cheek's Monokeratic system." " Monokeratic " is a Greek word, and means " the
unicorn." Cheek's system is the unicorn system.
That is the principle on which he does business
and realises a great fortune.'

' What is the unicorn system ? '

' The system of ready money. Most tradesmen have two systems—the cash system and
the credit system, and they do business on
both. Cheek does solely ready-money business.'

' So do others, but they don't call it by so
wonderful a name.'

' Exactly, and that is why they don't make
it answer so well. It is *because* Cheek calls a
simple thing by a sounding name that he does
a roaring trade. You know nothing, Joanna,
worth calling knowledge if you do not know
this, that English people love humbug as Italians
love oil and Spaniards love garlic. Nothing goes
down with them in politics, religion, business,
unless it be seasoned to rankness with humbug.
Mr. Cheek is sufficiently man of the world
to know that, and sufficiently clever to take
advantage of it. If old Joe Cheek did as
others, and sold for tenpence cash what his
neighbours sold for a shilling credit, he would

not have many customers, but he has managed very cleverly. Every article is priced at credit value, and when a customer leaves his shop he is given a cheque for the discount. He pays full credit price as cash, and receives the discount back as a cheque to be deducted from his bill when next he purchases at Cheek's. Do you understand? By this means he secures the return of the customer, who thinks he must come back and buy something more so as to recover the money on his cheque.'

'But if he does not go back?'

'Then he forfeits it. He has paid credit price in cash. This is the Monokeratic principle of business. You have no idea what a fascination the name and the cheque exercise on simple people.'

'But what has this to do with the unicorn?'

'Nothing whatever. The unicorn has one horn, and Cheek one way of doing business. That is the connection of ideas. The great charm lies in the word "Monokeratic," of the meaning of which the purchasers have not the smallest idea.'

'And he does a good business?' asked Joanna interested.

'A roaring business. I wish I did one-half as good. I lent him money when starting; but I knew my man. He slipped out of my fingers very quickly.'

'He must have brains,' said Joanna with admiration.

'He has indeed.'

'Then Mr. Charles is his son?'

'Yes—without the brains.'

'Is he in the business?'

'Oh dear no! Charlie is far too fine a gentleman to soil his fingers with trade. He can spend money, but cannot make it. Old Joe Cheek was very anxious to have his son in the concern. His idea is not bad. The old man is a Dissenter and a Radical, and he wanted Charlie to become a Churchman and Tory. Then he calculated each could milk his own cow. But Charlie had not the pluck and energy for it. There is where we Jews have the pull over you Christians. Now and then you have among you a man of genius who makes a business, but the son has not his ability or perseverance, and lets it fall. With us the faculty of business is transmitted hereditarily, like our features; it never fails, leaps a generation, dies out.'

' And Mr. Charles—what does he do with his time?'

' Throws it away. Faculties? Throws them away. Money? Throws it away. He has come to me for money, and I have helped him. The old man turns rusty at times; but everything must go to Charlie in the end, as he is the only son; and then the business also will be thrown away.'

' I suppose,' said Joanna, ' if he be such a fool, he may even throw himself away?'

Lazarus looked at her in surprise. ' You are clever,' said he, ' but not clever enough to manage that. The thing you must consider is, to keep yourself secure. I don't want to lose you as I lost——'

' Lost what?'

' Rachel.'

' Who ran away with Rachel?'

' Never mind. No one you ever heard of.'

' Where is she now?'

' I have told you I do not know.'

' Is she alone?'

' I do not know.'

' Is he with her?'

' No.'

'I suppose,' said the girl, 'if the burglar had cut your throat to-night, that Rachel would have heard of it, and come and claimed everything—your money, your jewels, your plate—and turned me out penniless.'

The Jew was startled, and looked at Joanna speechlessly.

'You have never been legally divorced?'

'No. I don't fling money among lawyers. We are separated for ever practically, though perhaps not legally.'

'Then she could take everything you have —or had, supposing your throat cut?'

'I suppose so,' was his slowly uttered reply, and he rubbed his legs before the fire, frowning and studying the coals.

'Joanna,' he said, after consideration of some minutes, which she did not interrupt, 'that shall never be. Rather than that I will bequeath everything to you, every stick in the storerooms, and crumb in the larder, and farthing in my chest.'

'That is your most sensible course,' said Joanna; 'that suits me better than stale advice and flat Ems.'

'I will do it,' said the Jew. 'I will write to Crudge.'

'I will bring the pen and ink at once.'

'Not now—there is time. I'll do it some time.'

'That will not suit me,' said Joanna. 'What has to be done must be done on the spot. Do you not see that your interests are at stake? You secure me in the shop, ensuring my caring for everything as if it were my own, protect yourself against peculation by me,' she laughed mockingly. 'You tie me to you as a faithful servant for ever. I shall no more grumble. I shall be active, and on the alert to drive hard bargains. I shall be bound to you Monokeratically.'

'What do you mean? How Monokeratically?'

'By one principle, the strongest of all—self interest.'

CHAPTER XV.

WANTED, A HOUSEMAID.

A FEW days after the events related in the fore-going chapters, Lazarus plunged into the kitchen with the newspaper in his hand, in hot excitement.

'Joanna!' he exclaimed, 'my dear Joanna, put down the saucepan at once, and follow me into my room. I have something very particular to say. Providence is playing into our hands. Look at the paper, read that!'

He thrust it towards her.

'My hands are wet,' she said; 'I cannot take the paper without reducing it to pulp. Read what you want me to know; I can listen and scour the saucepan.'

'You cannot. I want your close attention. Put down the pan. Here, come into my room, away from the distractions of a kitchen. Take a seat. I have much to explain to you. Now, at last, you may render me valuable service.'

'I have rendered you that for many years. I have recently saved your house from fire and your throat——'

'Do leave my throat alone; you are continually making allusions to it which are painful.'

Joanna followed him into his room, and wiped her hands on her apron. He held the sheet to her, and indicated the lines she was to read. The paper was a Plymouth daily newspaper of local circulation, widely distributed in the West of England. The Jew had indicated the advertisement columns.

'Well,' said Joanna, 'this does not concern me. "Wanted, a housemaid, immediately, in a gentleman's family; steady, experienced, not under twenty, a churchwoman; must have good recommendations. Wages, 16l. Apply, Mr. C. Worthivale, Court Royal Lodge, Kingsbridge."'

'It does concern you.'

'Only so far as to show me how little I get working for you. I am not going into service elsewhere—no such luck.'

'But I do want you to go into service with the advertiser.'

'What! Leave you?'

'Yes, for three months; then to return.'

' Why so ? '

' I will give you my reasons presently.'

Joanna looked again at the advertisement with a puzzled face.

' I am a maid-of-all-work. I am not an experienced housemaid, fit to go into a gentleman's family.'

' That does not matter. There is no mistress —no lady in the house to see if you do your work well or badly. Gentlemen do not care how they pig.'

' Steady,' said Joanna thoughtfully ; ' I am steady as the Eddystone, but I am not more than seventeen, and the advertiser requires a servant to be over twenty.'

' That does not matter. Gentlemen are no judges of the ages of ladies. Besides, you look old for your years.'

' A churchwoman,' mused Joanna ; ' I am nothing ; I have not been to any place of worship except the board school, and there we worshipped the inspector. How can I say I am a churchwoman when I've been neither to church nor chapel ? '

' That does not matter,' answered the Jew. ' It is all a matter of sitting and standing. When church does one thing chapel does contrary. Go to church for a Sunday or two, and you'll get enough scrape of ideas to pass muster.'

'Then, how about references? I do not suppose a character from you will count heavy.'

'I do not suppose it will,' answered the Jew. 'I'll get Mrs. Delany to give you one, the wife of Colonel Delany—a tip-top respectable party that.'

'She has never seen me.'

'That don't matter. I have lent her money.'

Presently Lazarus said, 'Go to the table, Joanna, and we will rough out a character for Mrs. Delany to put in form and write in her best hand.'

Joanna took a pen, dipped it in the ink, and drew a sheet of old dirty letter-paper before her. 'Go ahead,' she said, somewhat sulkily.

' " Mrs. Delany presents her compliments to Mr. C. Worthivale, and begs to recommend a strong, healthy young woman who has been in her service three years, with whom she would not have parted on any consideration had not the girl been called to nurse a dying mother." '

'No,' said Joanna, putting down her pen, 'I will not write that.'

'It is as true as the rest.'

'That is not what I scruple about. I will

not have my mother mentioned. She may be back any day with my ticket and ten shillings.'

'Very well,' said the Jew, 'then we will make it " white swelling." No—that won't do. Say, " domestic affliction." '

'Domestic affliction,' repeated Joanna after her dictator.

' " When released," ' continued Lazarus, ' " Mrs. Delany had supplied her place, and could not in conscience dismiss her new housemaid." '

'Go on,' said the girl. 'I have written as far as " housemaid." '

'Full stop after " maid," ' said the Jew. 'Begin again with a capital. " Mrs. Delany has always found the girl Joanna steady, conscientious, and hard-working; very clean, both in her person and her work; and, though young-looking for her age, is turned twenty." '

'This is the first time you've said a good word for me,' muttered the girl, 'and now it is half lies. Shall I add " eats voraciously and grows at a gallop "?'

'On no account, my dear child. Continue writing from my dictation,' said the Jew; ' " Joanna is unable to read or write." '

Joanna laid down her pen. 'Why do you say that?'

'Because it is the best recommendation that can be given. It is as much as saying that you are a good servant. Besides, Mr. C. Worthivale will be less afraid of leaving about letters and account-books if he thinks they are unintelligible to you.'

'I have written after your dictation that I cannot write. Is that all?'

'Yes, that will suffice. I will take the letter to Mrs. Delany, and get her to transcribe and post it—and put the penny stamp on also. You are sure of the situation.'

'You have not told me yet why I am to take it.'

'I will tell you now. Mr. Christopher Worthivale is steward to the Duke of Kings-bridge. I have advanced a great deal of money on the property of the Duke—more money than was prudent to put in one bag. The estate is so hampered with mortgages, and the requirements of the Duke are so great, that Court Royal must come to the hammer. The family is pretty well in my hands. I have the mortgage on the home estate, which is the same as a grip on their very heart. Now I want you to ascertain for me how matters really stand there. You must pry and discover. I want to know when to close the trap on the noble Duke, and whether I should leave it open a little longer. All the requisite information can be had at the steward's. You will have access to his office, and must look at his books. You are keen of wit as myself, and cunning at accounts as a banker's clerk.'

'I must give up my dancing lessons for this!' exclaimed the girl, pouting and disposed to cry.

'The dancing lessons! I had forgotten them.'

'I have not; nor Mr. Charles Cheek, and his suppers, and the rose silk dress, and the Roman pearls.'

'You shall have the lessons on your return.'

'By that time Mr. Cheek will have forgotten me.'

'That is possible.'

'But that does not suit me. *I will not go.*'

'I have my plans, Joanna.'

'And I have mine, Lazarus.'

He looked at her for some minutes, irresolutely. Her brow was clouded, her eyes dull;

the tears were filling them, and her lips quivered. She restrained the fall of the rain with
effort.

'Joanna, I am sending you where you may
observe the manners of the gentry. You are
sharp enough, and can use your knowledge.
You must study their habits of action and their
modes of speech. Some day you may have to
assume a position in which this knowledge will
be of service to you. Remember, you are my
heiress.' He opened a locked drawer, and drew
forth his will. 'Look! I have kept my word.
I have left everything to you. Now, in your
own interest it behoves you to see after my
investments at Court Royal. Look well at the
place. It may be yours some day. Such is
the way of the world. That which is at the
top comes down, and that which is at the
bottom mounts. It is so in every saucepan, in
every stew, and the world is but a boiling
cauldron where the currents cross one another
unceasingly.'

Joanna's face flushed, and the tears disappeared from her eyes, which waxed bright
and eager. 'I will go,' she said; 'I will do
everything you desire; I will find out everything.'

'Very well,' said Lazarus laughing. 'Now hunt up the sort of clothes you will need to wear, and let me see how you look in the rig-out of a respectable, sober-minded, and stupid English housemaid.'

After a few minutes she returned.

She had assumed a dark, quiet gown, with a white apron. She had brushed back her hair, and put on her a pretty white cap.

'Oh ho! on my word!' exclaimed the Jew. 'What sweet simplicity! Holloa, my pert Betsy Jane!' He chucked her under the chin insolently.

Joanna flushed crimson, and, striking him in the chest, sent him staggering back, to tumble over a stool and sprawl on the ground.

'I will do what you bid,' she said angrily, 'but touch me if you dare.'

Then the shop-door rang, and Joanna heard a voice calling her. She left Lazarus on the floor, rubbing his shin, and went into the shop. There stood Charles Cheek.

'Well now!' exclaimed the young man, 'this is a transformation scene in a pantomime. What is the meaning of this?'

'Mr. Cheek,' said Joanna, 'I have been considering what you said to me the other day.

I am going into another element, to learn the manners of the gulls. It is a voyage of discovery. I know no more of the habits and speech and thoughts of those I am going to see than if I were about to visit Esquimaux.'

CHAPTER XVI.

VENITE.

On the last day of November Joanna was deposited with her box at the gate of Court Royal Lodge. A servant came out, and helped her to carry the box round by the back door into the house. She was taken to her room, where she rapidly divested herself of her travelling clothes and assumed apron and cap. The fellow-servant looked critically at her, and said, ' Oh my ! how young you be ! How many sweethearts have you had ? Among them a redcoat, I reckon, if you've been in Plymouth. I should dearly like to have a redcoat. They be beautiful creatures.'

' I have no sweetheart,' answered Joanna.

' Then I reckon you won't be long without one here. There be gamekeepers here and the footmen. But of that another time. I tell you this is an easy place. There is no missus. There

R 2

ought to be proper-ly, but the young lady is
swallowed up by the folks at the Court, so she
is never here.   All the better for us.   Master
is a good sort of a man—very soft.   Lets us
have our own way, and believes all the crams
we tell.   As soon as you're ready the master 'll
want to see you.'

'I am ready now.'

'And,' continued the servant, 'I'll bet you
a shilling I know what he 'll say to y'.'

'I never bet.   Shillings are too hardly
earned to be cast away.'

'I didn't mean naught, really.   I'll tell y'
exactly what master 'll say.   He 'll begin like
the minister in church : " O come, let us worship, and fall down."   He always does with
every lady who comes into service here for the
first time.   There is his bell.   I reckon he won't
think you can be old enough, judging by your
looks.   I shouldn't believe you was twenty, if
you swore it till black in the face.'

Joanna was shown into the drawing-room,
where Mr. Worthivale stood on the mat, with
his back to the fire, moving his feet uneasily.
He disliked an interview with servants, not from
pride, but from consciousness that he was helpless in their hands—a defenceless fort.

'Good day,' he said; 'please shut the door. Miss Worthivale is not here at present, so I must tell you what you have to do. Your name is Joanna?'

'Yes, sir.'

'And your age is twenty?'

'So I am told, sir. I don't remember my birth.'

'I suppose not. Of course not. You are highly recommended to me. Mrs. Delany is the wife of Colonel Delany, of the Royal Engineers, I presume. One cannot make too sure. I turned up the name in the Directory. I understand you have suffered a domestic affliction. I see you wear a black gown. I am sorry. I hope you have not lost a very near relative—not a father or a mother?' He spoke in a kind, sympathetic tone.

'My father is dead, sir,' she answered, looking down and slightly colouring.

'Dear me—how sad! and your poor mother is alone in the world—a rough world for a fresh-bleeding heart to battle with. Have you brothers and sisters?'

Joanna answered, in a low voice, 'None, sir.'

'It must have been a hard matter for your

poor widowed mother to make up her mind to part with you. Sad also for you to have to leave her in her bereavement and desolation. Well, you have the comfort of knowing that a Hand is extended over the widow and the fatherless. Don't cry, child.'

Joanna was strangely agitated. The kind tone touched her, conscious of, and beginning to be ashamed of, her false position. Her cheeks darkened and her eyes clouded. She hung her head to conceal her face.

'You must write to your mother by this evening's post. Tell her you have arrived here quite safely, and—I think you may add you are in a house where you will be treated with consideration. Oh! I forgot — you cannot write. I beg you a thousand pardons ; it had escaped me. Shall I drop your mother a line? It would comfort her. Or, if you prefer it, get your fellow-servant, Emily, to write. I will let you have paper and envelope and stamp from the office shortly.'

'Thank you, sir,' said Joanna, looking up. She had recovered herself. 'My mother—I do not know where she is. She is not dead, but lost !'

'Good God !—-poor child !—Lord bless

me !—what tragedies are played in the depths
below the surface on which we swim serene !
But, for the matter of that,' he added with a
sigh, ' there are sad enough stories, cares, and
breakdowns about and above us. I suppose
happiness and sorrow are pretty equally distributed through all the strata of life—only
differing in kind, hardly in intensity. You look
very young, my child; I should not have
thought you as old as Mrs. Delany affirms.'

'I have had more experience than many
who are much older.'

'I have no doubt about that. Trouble and
responsibility ripen the character prematurely.
Sit down, Joanna ; you must be tired with
your long journey. I hope Emily has given
you something to eat. The drive from the
station is long and cold, over exposed moor.
Lord bless me ! when shall we have a junction
line ? '

'Thank you kindly, sir, I am not hungry.
The cook is going to give me some dinner
presently.'

'That is right. I will not detain you long.
I must put you in the way of things at the
outset, and then all will go smoothly afterwards. I dare say your attention was called

to a wall for nearly two miles along the roadside?'

'Yes, sir.'

'Very fine trees on the other side. Unfortunately, the trees are not now in leaf, so that they do not show to advantage. I always think that a park tree in winter is like a man of family without a landed estate. You know he is great, but he does not look it.'

'I saw the trees, sir.'

'Well, Joan. That is your name, is it not? The wall encloses the park, and the trees you saw grow in the park enclosed by that wall.'

'Yes, sir, I understand.'

'The park covers nearly—not quite—a thousand acres, and some of the timber is magnificent.' After a pause, to allow of the absorption and assimilation of what he had communicated, Mr. Worthivale said slowly, 'That park is Court Royal.'

'Does it belong to this house, sir?' asked Joanna, with affected simplicity.

Mr. Worthivale fell back against the mantelshelf, dropped his coat-tails, which must have touched the bars of the grate, as an odour of singed wool pervaded the room. 'Good heavens! what are you thinking of? You

must indeed be ignorant, very ignorant, to suppose that so magnificent a park could belong
to this humble residence. This house is Court
Royal Lodge. Not, you understand, the lodge
at the park gates, but an ornate cottage situated on a patch of ground cut out from the
park, where was once an overgrown, ragged,
and unsightly bed of laurels. His Grace was
pleased to erect the lodge for my late father.
It is the house of the steward. I am the
steward.'

Yes, sir.'

' And the park and the land as far as you
can see—that is to say, almost all, not quite all
—belongs to his Grace the Duke of Kingsbridge. I am the steward of his Grace. Now
you understand my position.'

' Yes, sir, and I am to be housemaid to the
steward of his Grace the Duke of Kingsbridge?'

' Quite so,' said Mr. Worthivale; ' you have
grasped the situation. Bless my soul! I have
burnt my tail. I thought I smelt something.
How can I have done that? Now, what I
want you particularly to understand, Joan,
from the outset is this—the proper manner in
which to address those of the ducal family who
do me the honour of calling. As it happens,

one or other comes here nearly every day. You, of course, have not had to do with people of title at Mrs. Delany's?'

'Mrs. Delany's husband is a colonel, sir.'

'A colonel!' echoed Mr. Worthivale, looking offended and disgusted. 'What is a colonel? Nothing.'

'Then,' continued Joanna, running over the uniforms in Mr. Lazarus's store with a mental eye, 'there was a field-marshal, and an admiral of the Blue, and half a dozen generals, and a silk cassock, red hood, and college cap.'

The steward silenced her with a wave of the hand.

'What I particularly wish you to understand, Joan, from the beginning is how you are to comport yourself at the door should his Grace, or Lord Edward, or Lord Ronald, or the Marquess, or Lady Grace ring the bell. Emily and you will have alternate afternoons at home. She likes to go out every other day, and I dare say you will be glad to do the same; exercise and fresh air are good for health. When Emily is out you will answer the bell. Open that photographic album on the table, and look at the first carte-de-visite—no, cabinet-size portrait. You perceive a venerable gentleman with white hair and fine aristocratic countenance. That is the Duke. He does not come here often. He cannot walk so far. If he comes, the carriage brings him. You cannot mistake him if you observe his waxlike complexion, and if you notice that the carriage stands at the gate. It is essential that you make no mistake in addressing him. I could pardon a lapse with the others, but not with him; so impress his features on your memory. When you open the door to him, mind you curtsey. Can you curtsey? The art is dying out. Ask Emily to put you in the way, and practise it till you are proficient. You must address the Duke as " your Grace." He will probably say, " My child, is Mr. Worthivale at home ? " Then you curtsey a second time and say, " Yes, your Grace." If I am out—which God forbid !—then say, " No, your Grace." If you are uncertain, say, " Will it please your Grace to step in, and I will inquire." You understand ? '

'Yes, sir.'

'Turn the page, and you will see two dignified gentlemen. One is Lord Ronald, the other Lord Edward. Look at them well. They are like the Duke, but have not quite his

presence and beauty. They are his brothers—
younger brothers, of course—which accounts for
their slight inferiority ; of course, I mean relative—relative only to his Grace. You address
them each as " my lord." " Is Mr. Worthivale
at home?" " Yes, my lord," or "No, my lord,"
as the case may be. Here, Joan, I will go
into the passage and knock at the door. Then
you open and curtsey, and I will represent—I
am ashamed to do it—the Duke of Kingsbridge, and you will receive me according as I
have instructed you. Let me see if you have
taken the lesson to heart. After that I will
represent Lord Ronald or Lord Edward. Let
me have the satisfaction of knowing that you
have apprehended my instructions.'

So Mr. Worthivale rehearsed with Joanna
what he had taught her. He was void of
all sense of humour, and unconscious of the
absurdity of his conduct, and that the girl was
laughing in her sleeve.

'Turn the page again,' said the steward.
'You see the Marquess. You address him also
as " my lord." You understand?'

'Yes, sir,' said Joanna distractedly. She
was looking at the next portrait with interest.
'Oh, sir ! please, sir, who is this beautiful lady?'

'That lady is as perfect and sweet in mind and soul as she is in feature,' answered Mr. Worthivale. 'That is the Lady Grace Eveleigh. And, remember, she is not Lady Grace, but *the* Lady Grace. A Knight's wife is a Lady, you know. *The* makes all the difference in the world. Everyone who knows that lady loves her, she is so good, so kind.'

'I am sure they do,' said Joanna eagerly. 'I am certain I shall love her, too.'

The steward was pleased; he smiled and nodded. 'You will address her as " my lady," you understand?'

'Yes.'

'Turn the page again, and you will see a photograph of Court Royal.'

'That house?' inquired the girl; 'why, it has got pillars before the door just like the Royal Hotel at Plymouth.'

Mr. Worthivale shuddered and drew back.

'My good girl! For heaven's sake don't liken a ducal mansion to—an—an—inn, however respectable and old-established. It is possible that the Royal Hotel may have a portico——'

'It has two,' said Joan, eager for the credit

of the Plymouth house. 'Has this place got two? I only see one in the picture.'

Mr. Worthivale was silenced; he coloured, and looked down on the rug, frowning. Court Royal had but one portico. Presently he said in an embarrassed tone, 'It may be true—I do not dispute it—that the inn in question has two porticos. But there is a difference, my girl, between porticos. Some are shams, shabby, and stucco; two, even five, porticos would be insignificant beside one real portico, such as that which graces the front of Court Royal. The pillars are of granite, red granite from Exmoor. When your eyes rest on the mansion you will feel at once the temerity of drawing comparisons between it and—and—an inn. Upon my word, I think you had better go there at once—that is, after you have had something to eat and drink. By the way, do not speak of the mansion as "the house;" that is scarcely respectful, and is contrary to usage. You mention it always as "the Court." You shall go down, Joan, to the Court after you have partaken of some refreshment. I will write a note which will serve as an excuse for sending you. When there, ask to see the housekeeper, Mrs. Probus, a most admirable woman. She will show you over the state apartments. His Grace is out. He has gone for a drive. I saw the carriage pass half an hour ago, and unquestionably the Lady Grace is with him. Lord Edward is away, back at his Somersetshire living, superintending the preparations for Christmas and the charities. The Marquess, I have no doubt, is out shooting, and you are not likely to come across Lord Ronald. Mrs. Probus knows what to do and where to take you. Rely upon her. Do not put off your walk too late. The days close in rapidly, and I want you to see the Court to advantage, and to be impressed by the influences of the Place and the Family.'

CHAPTER XVII.

STOCK-TAKING.

JOANNA was given the letter by Mr. Worthivale,
and walked through the park to Court Royal.
The evergreen shrubs on both sides of the drive
relieved the monotony of winter bleakness.
The pines were clothed; of them there was
great variety. The oak, though turned brown,
was not divested of all its leaves. The day was
fine and the air mild. Joanna knew nothing of
the country; she was surprised at and delighted
with all she saw. She stood watching the
fallow deer, till she was frightened by the rush
past her, on wing, of a pheasant. The wood-
pigeons were flying in hundreds from one beech
clump to another, rejoicing over the fallen
masts. The afternoon sun shone yellow over
the front of Court Royal, making the windows
glitter like sheets of gold leaf. Joanna went
round to the back of the house, and delivered

her letter and message. She was taken into the servants' hall, where some of the maids were receiving visitors from Kingsbridge, and stuffing them with veal pie, ham, tarts and clotted cream. They ate cream with their ham, heaped it on their bread, and jam on top of the cream equally deep ; they drank it with their tea, and filled the cups with lump sugar till the lumps stood out of the tea like Ararat above the flood. Some of the servants' friends had brought their children with them ; these over-ate themselves, were unwell, retired, and came back to repeat the process.

Joanna looked on in amazement. She was invited to take her place with the rest, but declined, as she had dined recently.

Then the housekeeper came in, smiled benevolently on the visitors, bade them enjoy themselves, and called Joanna away to see round the Court.

The housekeeper had been bred in the traditions of the knowledge and love and fear of the great Kingsbridge family. Her father had been a footman, her mother a lady's maid in the service of the late Duke, who had married and kept the lodge. The first recollection of her infant mind was being noticed as a healthy, pretty child, by the late Dowager Duchess. She had been educated, gratis, at the school supported by his Grace, a school which had in its window the ducal arms and supporters in stained glass, and outside, in the gable, the ducal coronet and initials of Beavis, seventh Duke of Kingsbridge. At an early age she had served the family by opening the gates of the drive, and had worshipped the family with curtsies before she had been found old enough to go to church and worship God. Then she had been taken into the Court, and been a servant there all her life, first in one capacity, then in another, till she married the red-faced coachman, who wore a white wig and sat on a hammercloth emblazoned with the ducal arms. Upon the death of the coachman, Mrs. Probus returned to the great house as housekeeper. It was unnecessary for her to do so. She had saved, during her long service, a good deal of money. The pickings had been considerable. But the pickings were too considerable, the living too good, the work too light to be resigned hastily, and Mrs. Probus felt that it would be banishment to hyperborean night to be consigned to an almshouse for the rest of her days, away from the splendour of the ducal

system, illumined only by the flicker of consciousness that the almshouses had been founded
for the reception of worn-out ducal retainers.
So, though Mrs. Probus often spoke of retiring,
she postponed the evil day.

Her little sitting-room, into which she introduced Joanna, was furnished with memorials
of the Eveleighs. Over the chimney-piece, of
course, was the portrait of the present Duke;
over the sideboard, the picture of the late Duke.
On the cheffonier were the silver tea-kettle given
her by the Duke on her marriage, and a silver
salver with a long inscription, presented to the
late lamented coachman on his completion of the
fiftieth year of service. On all sides were presents—remembrances of the Dowager Duchess
Anna Maria, of the late Duchess Sophia. On
her bosom she bore a brooch containing the
hair of the Marquess and Lady Grace, whom
she had nursed as infants; and about her finger
was a white ring woven of silver hair, cut from
the head of Frederick Augustus, sixth Duke of
Kingsbridge, Marquess of Saltcombe, Viscount
Churchstowe, Baron Portlemouth, Baronet,
Grand Commander of the Bath, Knight of the
Garter, of Saint Patrick, of the Black Eagle,

etc. etc. etc., cut off his head when she had laid him out for burial.

Mrs. Probus was proud to show the house to Joanna. When she learned that Joanna was the new servant come to the lodge, she understood at once that she had been sent down there to be impressed, and Mrs. Probus was never happier than when stamping the ducal family on young minds. A reverent fear and love of the family was the best preservative youth could have against the trials and temptations of life. It would save a girl from flightiness. Every one who moved in the Kingsbridge system was respectable to the tips of little finger and little toe. Imprudence was impossible to one nurtured in the Kingsbridge atmosphere. When the butler heard of a young man who had taken to drinking and gone to the bad, ' Poor fellow,' he said, ' if only he could have been received as a stableboy here ! ' When the housekeeper was told of a young woman who had lost her character, ' How dreadful ! ' she exclaimed ; ' would that she had been kitchen-maid at Court Royal ! ' As the monks and nuns of old believed that salvation was hardly possible outside the cloister, the domestics in the Kingsbridge constellation held that

no one went to hell from Court Royal or Kingsbridge House, Piccadilly. The same feeling
pervaded the entire estate. The tenants were
steeped in it. They were all respectable; the
farmers Conservative, churchgoers, and tem-
perate; their wives clean and rosy-cheeked,
attending to their dairies themselves, and curt-
seying like schoolgirls, and standing with their
hands under their aprons, when visited by one
of the family. The cottagers reared their
children to abstain from evil and do that which
is good, because there was a great Duke far
above them who knew everything that went on
upon his estates, and who, if the children were
clean and respectable, would take them up into
service in the Great House, and provide for
them and make them happy for ever.

No more moral, respectable, orderly, religious people were to be found in the West
of England than those on the Kingsbridge
estate; but all this morality, respectability,
order, and religion rested on the foundation
of the love and fear of the Duke. One Sunday, when the Rector's wife was catechising
the school children, she inquired who were
'the elect people of God,' whereupon they
responded, as with one voice, 'The tenants of

the Duke, ma'am.' And what they said they believed.

Mrs. Probus took Joanna up the grand staircase, turning and glancing at her face at the landings, to see that the proper expression of wondering awe was there. She bade her look at the pictures, and narrated the hackneyed story of their acquisition on the continent by the great Duke who was a general in the reign of George I. The keen eyes of the girl were in every corner, not on the pictures, which she did not understand, but on the cabinets, the Chinese vases, the pile carpet, the exotic ferns. In the state drawing-room she made a halt, and caught her breath.

'O my goodness!' she gasped; 'the Chippendale!'

'The *what?*'

'The Chippendale!' exclaimed Joanna. 'What first quality chairs and tables and cabinets. Why, they are worth a pot of money, just now that the fashion runs on Chippendale.'

'Of course the furniture is valuable,' said Mrs. Probus with dignity. 'But pray do not speak of it as though it were about to be sold at an auction.'

'And the china!' cried Joanna excitedly.

'That pair of Sèvres vases any dealer would give a hundred pounds for, and ask for them two hundred and fifty, and take two hundred.'

'No doubt the vases are precious. They were given to the late Duke by King Charles X. from the royal manufactory.'

'That nude figure of a woman seated on a dolphin is fine,' said Joanna. 'Oh, please may I look at the mark? Double C crowned—Ludwigsburg, modelled by Ringler. Look at the glaze. Observe the moulding!'

'It is scarcely delicate,' said Mrs. Probus.

'On the contrary, it is most delicate, and considering the delicacy, in admirable condition. Only some of the flowers on the pedestal are chipped.'

'I did not allude to the fragility of the china, but to the impropriety of a lady going about with only a scarf over her. However, the subject must be right, or it would not be here.'

'Of course it is right,' said Joanna excitedly. 'It is splendid; worth thirty pounds to a dealer, double to a purchaser. That is a pretty First Empire clock.'

'It don't go,' said Mrs. Probus.

'Who cares for that?' answered Joanna.

' The shape is the thing. The ornaments are very chaste. There you have some old Plymouth.'

' You seem to know a great deal about porcelain.'

' I do know something.'

' Ah, you ought to see the collection the Marquess has in his room. He is a fancier, and does not care what he pays to secure a piece to his taste.' The housekeeper was gratified at the enthusiasm and delight of the girl.

' May I—oh, may I see it ? '

' Let me see—the Marquess has gone out. I think it would be possible, though not allowed. We may not show strangers over the private apartments inhabited by the family. Still, this is a different case ; you are a servant, almost, I may say, of the family, as you are in the house of the steward. Follow me through the diningroom. I must show you the Rubens and Ostades and Van Dycks, and the Murillo bought by the late Duke Frederick Augustus ; he gave for it seven thousand pounds.'

Joanna sighed. ' I am ashamed to say I know nothing of the value of pictures. That requires a special education, which I have not had. It is a branch of the business——' She stopped abruptly, and then said, 'I dare say you have a catalogue of the paintings, which you could let me have. I should so much like to know what you have here; what to admire. Then, on another occasion, I shall be better able to enter into the merits of the pictures. You see, ma'am, with so much that is wonderful about one, the mind becomes bewildered. I will not look at the paintings to-day, I will look only at the china and the furniture.'

'Certainly,' said the housekeeper, 'what you say is just. I will give you a printed catalogue—privately printed, you understand.'

'That is a magnificent inlaid Florentine cabinet,' said Joanna; 'worth a hundred guineas. Oh, what treasures you have here!'

'Treasures indeed,' said Mrs. Probus; 'you see their Graces the Dukes of Kingsbridge have always been patrons of art, and have collected beautiful things in their travels through Europe.'

'If only there were to be a sale here——'

'Sale!' exclaimed the housekeeper; 'good heavens above! What do you mean? Sale! —sale in a ducal mansion! Young woman, restrain your tongue. The word is indecent.'

She tossed her head, frowned, and walked

forward stiffly, expressing disgust in every rustle of her silk gown and in the very creak of her shoes.

'I beg your pardon, ma'am. I was dazzled, and did not know what I was talking about.'

'Oh,' said Mrs. Probus, 'that alters the case. Now we are in the wing containing the private apartments. Here everything is more modern and comfortable. You admire the flowers, I perceive. Yes, there are camellia and ferns in the corridor. If you like it, I will conduct you over the conservatories—not now —presently. His Grace sets great store on the green-houses and winter-garden.'

'Dear ma'am, I should so greatly like to see them. I love flowers above everything in the world. I have only five little pots at home, on the roof, and one of them contains a bit of wild heather I dug up with my scissors, on the rare occasion of a holiday. Now that I am away, I do not know who will attend to my poor plants, and whether I shall find them alive when I return. I have no one in the world whom I can ask to do a thing for me.'

'This is the apartment of Lord Ronald,' said the housekeeper. 'I will not show you in there. It contains nothing of interest—that is, nothing very extraordinary. His lordship was a soldier, and loves to have everything plain. No doubt it contains much that would interest military men, but such as you and me don't understand those pursuits. Here is the Marquess's door. Wait a moment, whilst I tap and peep in to make sure he is out. I am sure he went out shooting, I saw him with the keeper and the dogs—that is,' she corrected herself, ' I saw the keeper and the dogs with him.'

Mrs. Probus tapped timidly, and then opened. ' Look about you,' she said, ' at the costly china. He is out, as I supposed. It is very bold of me to enter and introduce you. See what abundance of porcelain there is here. The Marquess is most particular. He will not allow the housemaids to touch it. When dusty, Lady Grace takes it down and cleans it. He allows no other fingers than hers to touch his valuable collection.'

' How pretty the flowers are,' said Joanna, looking at the bouquets on the table and on the chimney-piece. ' So many posies—and specimen glasses everywhere.'

' Lady Grace always arranges them for her brother,' answered the housekeeper.

'No wonder that they are lovely,' said the girl. 'I should so much like to see Lady Grace.'

'You will do so some day. Yes,' she said, as she saw that Joanna was looking at a miniature on the wall over the fireplace, 'that is her ladyship when she was younger—when she was about eighteen.'

Joanna looked at the portrait with interest for a long while. Reluctantly, at last, she turned away and began to examine the china.

'This is Chelsea,' she said contemptuously, 'bad of its kind.'

'It cannot be bad,' protested Mrs. Probus, 'or it would not be here.'

'This group——' began Joanna, putting forth her finger.

Mrs. Probus arrested her hand. 'For heaven's sake do not touch. You might break —and then—dear life! I should sink through the floor in shame and sorrow.'

'I shall not break anything,' answered Joanna. 'I could walk like a cat among Dresden figures, or a best Swansea service, and not upset or injure one article. Besides, if that group were broken, what odds! It is a modern imitation.'

'What! a connoisseur among my china! Condemning it, moreover!'

Mrs. Probus turned, shivered through all the gathers of her silk gown, raised her hands deprecatingly, and turned pale.

Joanna looked round at the speaker and recognised the Marquess from the photograph she had been shown. She said, with perfect composure, 'Yes, my lord, this piece is not genuine. I can tell it by the colour of the glaze.'

'Indeed! I gave a long price for it.'

'You were taken in, my lord. It is not worth fifteen shillings.'

'Oh, my lord,' gasped Mrs. Probus, 'I beg your pardon ten thousand times. I thought you was out, and I dared take the liberty—the inexcusable liberty—of bringing this young person in, who pretended to be interested in porcelain—and her to dare and say your lordship was taken in! You'll excuse my audacity, my lord, I pray, and her ignorance and impertinence.'

'My dear Probus,' said the Marquess smiling, 'I am overpleased to have my collection shown to one who has taste and knowledge, and discrimination.' Turning to Joanna, he added, 'I believe, to my cost, that you are right. Doctor Jenkyn, who knows more about china than anyone else in this county, has pronounced unhesitatingly against this piece. You are of the same opinion?'

'I know it, my lord. I know where it was made. There is a manufactory of these sham antiques. I can tell their articles at a glance.'

'You seem to have an accurate eye and considerable knowledge.'

'In my former situation I was with a master who collected china, and so I learned all about it—if I broke any, I got whacks.'

'Don't be so familiar,' whispered Mrs. Probus, greatly shocked.

'And,' continued Joanna, 'my master, after a while, so trusted my judgment, that he would let me spend pounds on pounds on porcelain for him.'

'Were you never taken in?'

Joanna laughed. *She* taken in! 'Never, my lord.'

'I should like to know your opinion of these bits of Chelsea.'

'I have already given it,' said Joanna, disregarding the monitions of the housekeeper. 'I told Mrs. Probus it was a lot of rubbish.'

The Marquess laughed.

'Right again. That is exactly Dr. Jenkyn's opinion, not expressed quite as forcibly as by you.'

'Here, my lord, you have a charming little Dresden cup and saucer; really good; canary yellow, with the cherubs in pink. It is well painted, and good of its kind.'

'Keep it,' said the Marquess. 'I make you a present of it as a remembrance of my den which you have invaded.'

'Thank you! thank you! this is kind,' said Joanna, with sparkling eye. 'I will never part with my little cup, never; and I beg pardon, my lord, for having persuaded Mrs. Probus to bring me in here, against her better judgment. It was not her fault, it was mine. I entreated her to let me see your china.'

'Not another word; you are heartily welcome. If I want to buy china again, I will consult you.'

Joanna withdrew with a curtsey. Lord Saltcombe signed to the housekeeper to remain behind.

'Who is the little china-fancier?' he asked, in a low tone.

'Oh, my lord! I am so ashamed. Only the new housemaid at the lodge.'

' Indeed! how education advances ! ' laughed the Marquess.   ' In the march of culture we are being overtaken.   Who would have supposed to find a housemaid so thorough a connoisseur ? Well, she looks brimming over with brains, she has plenty of assurance, and is deucedly pretty.'

27 3

CHAPTER XVIII.

LADY GRACE.

THE words of commendation spoken by the
Marquess were sufficient to make Mrs. Probus
think of Joanna with more favour than before.
She had recovered from her panic, Joanna had
cleverly taken all the blame on herself, so the
old woman's face was wreathed with smiles, and
she professed her readiness to show the girl
whatever she desired. The Marquess had pronounced on her abilities—a word of commendation from him was enough for Mrs. Probus.

'I dare say, my dear,' said she confidentially,
'that Mr. Blomfield, the butler, will let you see
the plate.'

'I am a judge of plate,' said Joanna gravely.
'I know the hall marks on silver as I do those
on china.'

'You do? Lord bless me!' exclaimed the
housekeeper. Well, what is education coming

VOL. I. T

to ? That shows his lordship was right. He said you had brains.'

'Did he ? Then he can judge people as I judge china. I should very much like to see the plate.'

Mr. Blomfield did not require much pressing; he was proud to show the splendour of the house in his department. He allowed Joanna to enter the plate room, and he opened for her the iron doors of the cupboards in the wall, and exhibited the shelves, lined with green cloth, on which shone centre-pieces, goblets, urns, tea and coffee pots, spoons and forks, salvers large and small, candlesticks and candelabra. All were in perfect order, shining brilliantly.

'This,' said Mr. Blomfield, opening another case, 'contains very old family plate. It is only brought out on the grandest state occasions. Here is a silver gilt ewer, magnificently chased, said to be three hundred years old; the present Duke was baptized out of it, but I believe it was a punchbowl formerly. Much of this is admired, but I cannot say I like it. The forks have but two prongs, and the spoons are rat-tailed. There is no accounting for the taste that can admire such things as these.'

'I suppose, sir, you have an inventory of all

the plate,' said Joanna timidly, raising her large dark eyes to those of the butler.

' Of course, miss, I have; and I go over it with the steward on occasions. Very proper it should be so, though a mere matter of form. You will not find many mansions where there is such choice of plate. There is a great salver which was presented to Field-Marshal John, Duke of Kingsbridge, when he was Lord Salt-combe, in King George's reign, by the mayor and citizens of Ghent. I've heard,' continued the butler, ' that in some of your parvenu families there is a lot of plate, a great and vulgar display—but the quality is not there. All this is old and fine, and in good style. The new plate looks to-dayish; there is not the character about it that our ancestral store possesses.'

' Do you know, sir, what you have got in each cupboard ? '

' Of course I do, miss. Do you not see that a list of the contents of each is pasted against the iron door, inside ? And with the list is the weight in silver and gold.'

' What is the weight of the whole amount of silver, Mr. Blomfield ? ' asked the housekeeper.

' I have never counted,' was his reply. ' It

is easily done ; sum the totals affixed to each list
on the doors.'

'I should dearly like to know,' said Joanna.
'Where I was before I came here there was a
good deal of plate ; but nothing like this, oh,
nothing !'

'I suppose not,' said Mr. Blomfield with
dignity. 'No one with a title, I suppose ? '

'Oh dear no. What about now, do you
think, sir, is the weight ? '

'I will take the numbers down and add them
up,' said Mrs. Probus good-naturedly.

'Excuse me, sir,' said Joanna ; ' you have a
very beautiful bread-basket there. Might I look
at it more closely, and see the hall-mark ? '

'Certainly.' He handed the basket to her.
Joanna looked at the handle. 'It belongs to
the reign of William and Mary. The year I
cannot say without a book.'

'Dear, now! To think you have found
that out! I have had to do with plate all my
life, and know nothing more of the marks than
to look for the lion and the head.'

'Here is the sum of the weight of plate,'
said Mrs. Probus. 'The silver in this column,
the gold in that.'

'All that ? ' exclaimed Joanna. 'Why, the

silver at six-and-six an ounce, without allowing anything for workmanship, is—five thousand ounces — sixteen hundred and twenty-five pounds; but it would sell at a pound an ounce. Five thousand pounds' worth of plate at the lowest.'

'You can calculate pretty quickly,' laughed the butler.

'The Marquess said she had brains,' said Mrs. Probus aside to Mr. Blomfield; 'he was quite taken with her cleverness.' Then to Joanna, 'Now I will show you over the conservatories. You may keep the sum of the plate if you like.'

'Thank you,' answered Joanna. 'I shall like it very much.'

Joanna was one of those children of this century, and of town civilisation, in whom shrewdness and simplicity, precocity and childishness, are strangely mixed together. When in the house among the furniture, china, and plate, she was reserved, observant, calculating, storing her observations in her retentive memory, prizing everything she saw; but when she entered the greenhouses, that calculating spirit left her, and she was an unspoiled girl, overflowing with fresh delight, full of exuberant

spirits.   In the house, amidst the artistic valuables, she was in a world with which she was
acquainted ; in the conservatories she had passed
to another and unfamiliar sphere. She had been
reared in the midst of manufactured goods, apart
from nature ; now she was introduced to nature's
best creations.   Mrs. Probus was amused at the
girl's expressions of rapture at the beauty of
what she saw.   Grapes she saw for the first
time hanging from the vines, and oranges shining among the glossy leaves of the trees, side by
side with silvery flowers.   The dwarf apricots
and nectarines were still burdened with fruit.

When she saw the flowers her excitement
was unbounded. She laughed and cried at once.
Her cheeks flushed, her eyes sparkled, hands
and feet were in incessant agitation.   The pri-
mulas, the cyclamen, were in full, delicate bloom.
The wax-like camellias, white and crimson, were
in flower; chrysanthemums, screened from frost,
were in tufts of every colour.   The air was
scented with white Roman hyacinths.

'Oh !' cried Joanna, with hands uplifted, 'I
would that the Barbican and all the world would
sink into the ocean, and leave me alone here,
to be happy with the flowers, for ever.'

At that moment the door from the next, the

orchid house, opened, and Lady Grace Eveleigh appeared, dressed in silvery grey, with a quiet, close bonnet on her head. She looked at the excited girl with a sweet, confidence-inspiring smile, and came forward.

'Dear alive, my lady!' exclaimed Mrs. Probus, 'I am a most unfortunate body to-day. I took the liberty of taking this young woman through the conservatories, without a thought that your ladyship was here. I have been unfortunate, indeed, this afternoon.'

'Not at all, not at all, Probus,' said Lady Grace. 'I am always delighted that others should enjoy our pretty flowers. You like flowers,' she added, turning to Joanna, her voice soft as the cooing of a dove.

'I love them,' said the girl, clasping her hands together.

'What were you saying as I came in?' asked Lady Grace.

Joanna answered, half laughing, half crying, 'I said that I wished the world would sink under the sea and leave me alone with the flowers.'

'That was rather a selfish wish,' said Lady Grace. 'Do you not care that others should share your pleasure?'

'No, not at all,' answered Joanna bluntly.

'Excuse her, my lady,' put in Mrs. Probus, with a frightened look, 'she doesn't mean really to differ from your ladyship ; she doesn't understand what she says.'

'I do ! hold your tongue,' said Joanna, turning sharply on the housekeeper.

'Do not trouble yourself, dear Probus. Whoever loves flowers has a kindred feeling with me. I love them with all my heart.' She looked at Joanna, who stood undecided what to say or do. Then, turning to Mrs. Probus, she said, 'Will you do me a favour, and yield your place to me, nurse? Let me take her round the houses. You do not know the pleasure it gives me to show the flowers to one who can feel towards them like myself.'

'Very well, my lady,' said the old woman, ' but you must not take it amiss—if this young person——'

'I shall take it greatly amiss,' interrupted the lady, ' if she does not admire what I admire. I can see in her bright eyes that she is happy with my pets. Leave us alone together ; we shall perfectly understand each other. We flower fanciers have a language of our own, understandable among ourselves, sealed to out-siders.'

When Mrs. Probus was gone, Lady Grace, looking kindly into the girl's excited face, asked, ' Will you tell me what is your name ? '

' Joanna.'

' Joanna ! ' repeated Lady Grace. ' That name is uncommon. It is pretty, very pretty, and quaint. I like it.'

The girl flushed with pleasure and pride.

' I am glad you like it,' she said; ' I never thought a button about my name before. Now I shall like it.'

' I hope you like Probus,' said the lady. ' She was my nurse long, long ago. She used to scold me a little and caress me a great deal.'

' Please, my lady,' Joanna spoke timidly, ' may I go very, very slowly along, because all this is so new and so beautiful that I cannot bear to miss anything ? Mrs. Probus walked so fast, and was afraid of staying long anywhere.'

' I will go as slow as you like, and stop as long as suits you beside any flower. That is a yellow primula ; look, under the leaves is white flour, it comes off on your finger, and that gives the plant its Latin name. It has a sweet scent. Whence do you come from, Joanna ? '

The girl pointed downwards.

The questioner looked at her with surprise, not understanding the significance of the indication.

'Out of the depths. Picked out of the mud —true as my word unvarnished,' explained Joanna.

'So is it with the water-lily,' said Lady Grace, 'one of the purest and most glorious of flowers. Its roots are in the basest slime, its flowers in the sunshine without soil. I am sure, Joanna, you will grow up as the water-lily.'

The girl shook her head. 'You don't understand. I am not a flower, but a grub.'

'And the grub becomes a butterfly, that soars far above the garbage on which it crawled and fed.'

'I can never be a butterfly.'

'You can rise.'

'I am rising,' said Joanna firmly; 'I intend to rise. But you think your way, and I think mine. You rise your way, which I cannot understand or copy, and I rise mine as I may, in whatever direction chance gives me an opening.'

Lady Grace looked into the girl's face and tried to decipher its language. She saw that

the mind was full of intelligence, precociously
developed. She saw that ideas were working
which Joanna was powerless to express. The
girl misunderstood the intent look of the lady,
and said, 'I have made you angry. Everyone
here is taught to agree with you. I say what
I think. Whether it jumps or jars with the
opinions of others matters little to me.'

'I like you to speak out of your heart freshly
what you think.'

'Then,' said Joanna eagerly, 'I think there
is not a flower in all this place so sweet and so
beautiful as you, lady.'

'You must not say that.' Lady Grace
coloured.

'Why not? It is true.'

'No, it is not true.'

'I think it.'

'Never mind. Do not speak such things. I
do not like them, and they will make me dis-
trust you.'

Both were silent for a few minutes, and then
Joanna said, 'How very, very happy you must
be here, my lady.'

'Yes,' answered the lady, in her soft, sweet
voice, in which was a tone of sadness, 'I am
happy.'

Joanna noticed the omission.

'Why do you not say *very* happy?

'I am indeed happy and thankful.'

Joanna now looked at her as intently as Lady Grace had previously observed *her*. The expression on Joanna's face was one of perplexity. At last she said, 'I don't understand, and I can't understand.'

'What, Joanna?'

'My lady, you do not and you cannot understand me, and I do not, and try as I may I cannot, understand you. We belong to different worlds.'

'And are forgetting the bond between us— the flowers.'

Presently Lady Grace pointed to an arcade, where, against the wall, oranges, limes, and citrons were growing.

'Do you notice these trees?' she said; 'they are very ancient, one or two of them are as much as two hundred years old.'

'What a pity!' answered Joanna; 'they must be worn out. You should stub them out and plant new, improved sorts.'

Lady Grace went into the vinery, and brought thence a large bunch of green Muscatel grapes on a leaf. She presented it, smiling, to Joanna.

'It is a pleasure,' she said, ' to have grapes for the sick and those who have no vineries of their own. They do enjoy them so greatly.'

'Do you give grapes away?'

'Yes, of course we do.'

'But you might sell them and make a lot of money—enough to pay the gardener's wage.'

Lady Grace coloured and laughed. 'We couldn't possibly do that.'

'Why not?'

'For one reason, because then we should have no grapes to give away.'

'But you are not obliged to give them away?'

'To the sick, of course we are.'

'Why of course?'

'Why, *because* they are sick.'

'They should buy grapes for themselves if they require them.'

'They are poor, and cannot do so.'

'Then let them do without. You are not bound to them, nor they to you.'

Lady Grace, with a little sadness on her brow, but a smile on her lips, said, observing her, 'It is a pleasure to give them what they cannot get themselves. There, it is a greater pleasure to me to watch you enjoying that bunch of Muscatel than if I were eating it myself.'

Joanna shook her head. 'We belong to different worlds,' she said. 'If these greenhouses were mine I would keep everyone out but myself, and I would spend my life in them, looking at the flowers and eating the grapes.'

'You would not spare me a bunch?'

'I would give you everything,' said Joanna vehemently.

'Why?'

'Because I love you, and would want to make you love me.'

'You ought to love the sick, the suffering, and the needy, and be ready to relieve them.'

'They are nothing to me. They can do nothing for me.'

'We are all one family, tied together by common blood, bound by mutual duties, members of one body; and the hand cannot say to the foot, "I have no need of you," nor the head to the hand, "I have no need of you."'

'We are individuals,' answered Joanna. 'To look out for self is the law of life and of progress. I have heard Laz—I mean my late master—say

that this it is which makes the United States so
great and prosperous, that every man lives as an
unit, cares nothing for his fellows, and beats his
way through and over all who stand in his path.
This it is which makes the old order fail, that
every man under it was entangled in responsibilities to every man around him, above, below,
and on his level, and was not free. The old
order *must* give way to the new. That is what
my master said.'

'I do not like your theory, Joanna. It grates
with my notions of right and wrong.'

'I dare say not, my lady. You have been
reared under the old principle of social life, I
under the new. Each man for himself, my
master said, is the motto of the coming age, and
those who are hampered with the old doctrines
of mutual responsibilities must go down.'

'You are a very extraordinary girl.'

'No, my lady, I am not. I am merely the
child of the period, a representative of the coming age ; there are thousands and ten of thousands like me, trained in the same school. To
us belongs the future.'

Lady Grace Eveleigh sighed, and put her
hand to her brow, unconsciously. 'I have no
doubt you are right,' she said ; 'I feel rather

than see that it is so. Yes—perhaps it is well.
I do not know. I suppose I am prejudiced. I
like the old order best.'

Joanna was frightened. She had spoken
too boldly ; not insolently, but confidently.
She feared she had hurt her guide. When
Lady Grace put her hand to her brow, it was
as though she had received a blow. Joanna
touched her.

' Was I rude? Have I pained you? I am
very, very sorry. I would die rather than hurt
you.' She caught Lady Grace's hand and
kissed it.

' No, not a bit,' answered the lady. ' It
does one good to know the truth. Sooner or
later it must be brought home to us, and rather
from your lips than from a ruder tongue. We
go on in a dream, with the poor always about
and with us, and will wake up with surprise to
find them above us. I hear my father and
uncles forecasting the future, with dismal faces ;
I did not expect to hear the same forecast ani-
mating the rising power. Do not let us talk
of that longer. Let us consider the flowers.
By the way, I suppose you will be at our
Christmas tenants' ball. We give one in the
winter to the farmers and their families, and to

the servants and their friends. Of course you will be there.'

'Oh, what a pity, what a pity, what a pity!''

Lady Grace was unable to refrain a laugh at the girl's exclamations and droll consternation.

'What is such a pity?' she asked.

'I was to have learned to dance, but my coming here interfered with my lessons, so I can only look on and not be able to take a part.'

'You shall have some lessons,' said Lady Grace Eveleigh, with a sweet, kind smile. 'I will see to that. Miss Worthivale will arrange what times will suit best, and you shall be taught by me, in my own room. Miss Worthivale is so good and sweet that she will help me.'

'Oh, thank you, thank you,' exclaimed Joanna; 'that is prime!'

'There is one thing more,' said the lady; 'as you are fond of flowers, I suppose you must have something like a garden at home.'

'I have five pots—one cracked, and an old teapot without a spout.'

'What grow in them?'

Fuchsias, Guernsey lilies, geranium, and wild heath.'

'Will you accept this from me? It is nothing to look at now; only a crowd of little horns poking out of the earth; but they will expand in time into lilies of the valley, full of beauty and fragrance. Keep them as a remembrance of me.'

'I will never, never part with them,' said Joanna. 'This is the second present I have had to-day. Look here! Your brother gave me this.' She showed the porcelain cup and saucer.

'Lord Saltcombe gave you that! What—have you been talking to and astonishing him?'

'Yes,' said the girl, 'I did astonish him a bit. He gave me this; but I like your flowers best.'

'I must leave you now; I saw my father return in the carriage.' Lady Grace hesitated a moment, looked questioningly at Joanna, and then touched her, drew her to her, and pressed a light kiss on her brow. 'We are travellers over one pass. Some ascend as others go down; as they meet and pass, they salute,' she said, and slipped away.

CHAPTER XIX.

SLEEPY HOLLOW.

The Venerable the Archdeacon of Wellington, Bachelor of Divinity, Canon of Glastonbury, Rector of Sleepy Hollow, and Chaplain to his Grace the Duke of Kingsbridge, was sitting in his study with his wife one morning in November, discussing the list of poor people to whom Christmas benefactions were to be given.

The Archdeacon regarded himself, and was regarded, as a man of business. He was secretary to several diocesan societies ; he was a stay to the Kingsbridge family. Whenever a spasm recurred in the financial condition of the Eveleighs, a telegram summoned him to South Devon, and he spent some hours in consultation with the steward at Court Royal. When he returned to Somersetshire he felt that his presence had been of use. So it had on more occasions than one, for he had advanced money to relieve the strain.

'Really,' said Lady Elizabeth Eveleigh—
—the Venerable the Archdeaconess, and Grey
Mare of Sleepy Hollow—'I think we do a
great deal more than is necessary. There are
the coal club, and the clothing club, and the
blanket club, and the shoe club, and the Sunday school club, and the widows' alms, and the
three yards of flannel to every married woman
in the place, and the Christmas largess and the
Christmas beef. This comes very heavy. You
cannot put our charities at a less figure than
sixty pounds per annum ; then that great im-
posture, Queen Anne's Bounty, absorbs sixty
pounds more, and the rates come to eighty,
and the curate gets one hundred and twenty-
five. Church expenses amount to ten pounds ;
the living is worth three hundred and forty
pounds—that leaves us just five pounds on
which to keep house, pay five servants, and
entertain all the neighbourhood, subscribe to
every church restoration, and contribute to
every bazaar.'

'My dear Elizabeth, I have my canonry.'

'Worth eight hundred pounds, which goes
into that Goodwin Sand, the Kingsbridge debt.
I know it does. Do not pull a face ; I know
it. I never finger the money.'

' Then there is my archdeaconry, worth two hundred.'

' Out of which we pay the servants and keep the carriage. Edward, it is really too bad; you ought to have been a bishop.'

' Elizabeth, how is that possible, with the Liberals in power ? '

' I am sure that ought to be no hindrance to your promotion. You have never offered an opinion decidedly on any topic, political or ecclesiastical, that could be objected to by any-one. You have been most tolerant. Your charities have been given indiscriminately to Dissenters and Church people. You never have taken a side. You have been scrupulously *via media.*'

' I do not want to be a bishop. I have not the physical strength.'

' I do. A bishopric means a good deal more than the four thousand set down in " Whitaker "—it means getting a haul out of Queen Anne, and some pickings, may be, from the Ecclesiastical Commissioners.'

' Let us return to the lists, Elizabeth. We are considering Betty Perkins, not me.'

' Betty Perkins puts me out of patience, said the Venerable the Grey Mare. ' She has only just paid into the clubs one lump sum. I cannot see the good of clubs and rules, if she is to be allowed to reap the benefit of the former whilst violating the latter. She has sent in four-and-fourpence for the coal club, four-and-fourpence for the clothing club, four-and-fourpence for the shoe club, four-and-fourpence for the blanket club, and twenty-one shillings and eightpence for her five children, who only attend Sunday school now and then—just before the treat and the Christmas tree. I have her money in my pocket now—listen how it rattles —thirty-nine shillings in all. She will get her cards with seventy-eight shillings on them, just thirty-nine shillings allowed her for putting in her money to-day, to receive it out with interest to-morrow. It is preposterous. I believe she borrowed the sum for the occasion. I refuse to be treasurer and secretary to the charitable clubs if you wink at such flagrant cases.'

'My dear Elizabeth, there is no one else in the parish capable of managing the clubs. As to Betty Perkins, consider how poor she is, with a husband given to drink, and five children.'

'Rules are rules,' said Lady Elizabeth.

' Yes, my dear, but justice must be tempered with mercy.'

' I do not think the clubs and alms do good The people take what is given them as a right. They are not grateful, they do not come to church a bit the better for being bribed at the rate of five pounds per house to come.'

' We cannot give up the clubs, Elizabeth. They really are a great comfort to the people.'

' You pauperise them, Edward. Well?' to the man-servant who appeared at the door ; ' what is it, Thomas?'

' Please, my lady, there is a gentleman in the drawing-room who wants to see his lordship.'

' Let me look at the card,' said the Archdeaconess. ' Rigsby ! Rigsby—I do not know the name. Some traveller for a wine merchant, I suppose.'

' Bless me !' exclaimed Lord Edward Eveleigh, when, by his wife's kind permission, he was allowed to look at the card ; ' my old college friend Rigsby. I thought he was in Ceylon, coffee-growing. I heard he had realised a great fortune. Excuse me, my dear Elizabeth. Settle Betty Perkins as you like— that is, no, let her off this time, and I will have a talk with her. She will be more regular next year. Elizabeth, I must ask Rigsby to lunch.'

'There is cold mutton and mince,' answered Lady Elizabeth: 'Also tapioca pudding.'

'I haven't seen Rigsby for forty years—no, not for forty years. I must insist on his paying us a visit. You can manage it, Elizabeth?'

'The sheets in the best bedroom are aired.'

The Archdeacon hastened into the parlour, where he found a tall brown man, with grey hair, seated, awaiting him.

'I am so glad—so delighted to see you again,' said Lord Edward, extending both hands.

'I have come,' said Mr. Rigsby, 'on my daughter's account. We have been visiting Glastonbury, and she has been taken ill there, whether with neuralgia or toothache it is not for me to determine. She is a sad sufferer—and I thought, being in a strange place, that I might venture on calling, trusting you might not have quite forgotten me——'

'My dear Rigsby——' interrupted the Archdeacon, with overflowing cordiality.

'Excuse me,' said the visitor, putting up his hand to stop him, 'I will say what I desire first, and then shall be thankful for your remarks on

it. I was observing that I relied on your kindness, which I well remembered, to help me
with your advice.   I am a stranger in Glastonbury, indeed a stranger in England. You have
a local dentist here—that is, at Glastonbury. I
want to know——'

'Vigurs is the man for you,' said Lord
Edward.

'One moment, and I have done,' continued
Mr. Rigsby, looking with impatience at the
Archdeacon. 'I have no confidence, myself,
in local practitioners; if there be real genius it
will unquestionably gravitate to town, and the
dregs of the profession be left in the country.'

'I beg your pardon——'

'You will allow me to finish what I was
saying.' Rigsby looked Lord Edward down.
'One hears atrocious stories of the misdeeds of
these men—breaking jaws, drawing the wrong
teeth, and so on. I could not suffer Dulcina to
run such a risk unless I were perfectly satisfied
that the man was really first-rate.'

'Vigurs is a splendid fellow; a thorough
Churchman, and always stays——'

'Excuse me if I say that this is neither here
nor there. I do not care a snap for the religion
and politics of Mr. Vigurs, but I do care for his

being a first-class dentist. It is a long way to town, and Dulcina's sufferings are so intense that I am inclined to place my sweet child in the hands of a man, even if in the country, if he may be trusted. I suppose that in Bath or in Bristol a dentist of some experience and intelligence——'

'I can assure you——'

'I shall have done directly. I was observing, when interrupted, that in Bath or Bristol a dentist of experience may be found, but that would entail a journey to Bath or Bristol. Dulcina, poor child, is so prostrated by her pains last night that I hardly like to move her so far. If you saw the sweet flower, you would say the same—so fragile, so fair, so languishing.'

'You may rely on Vigurs,' said the Archdeacon. 'He has drawn many of my teeth and stopped others. Vigurs is quite a first-rate man.'

'If the tooth be drawn, ether or nitrous oxide must be used. Can I trust this man to employ such means? My child's life is too precious to be played with. She is my only child, heiress to all the fortune I have toiled for forty years to gain. She will be worth ten thousand a year after I am gone. Judge if the world can do without one so gifted. As for me, I live only for Dulcina. Were she to expire under nitrous oxide I should blow out my brains.'

'Have perfect confidence in Vigurs. He is a man of note. This neighbourhood is well peopled with county families, and they all go to Vigurs in preference to London dentists. Where is your daughter now?'

'She is at the White Hart. Miss Stokes, her aunt, is with her. She has administered soothing drops, and Dulcina is asleep. Poor soul, she needs repose after the torture of toothache or neuralgia. I do not pretend to determine which it is, but she has a carious molar. I have seen it. You are positive that Mr. Vigurs may be allowed to look at my daughter's jaw?'

'Positive. First-rate man, gentle as a lamb with ladies. Now Rigsby, as your daughter is asleep, spare me a few minutes to tell me something about yourself. You look well burnt like a coffee berry, but hearty—more so than myself, who am but a creaking gate. Have you definitely left Ceylon?'

'Yes; Dulcina and I came here to look at a house and park that is for sale. Dulcina and I intend to settle in the country. I have sold my estates in Ceylon, providentially before the coffee disease invaded the island, so that I sold them well, and the purchaser, not I, has been ruined, for which I cannot be too thankful. We like this country, and this part of the country. It is rich, well wooded, and there seem to be many gentlemen's seats about. I cannot say that Shotley Park is quite to our taste, but we will think over it, and discuss it together when Dulcina's tooth ceases to distract her. Poor dear, she can give her attention to nothing now but her tooth and the nerve that runs up into the head across the cheek from the jaw.'

'Will you take anything?'

'I should not object to a glass of sherry and a biscuit. Nervousness about my daughter has rather shaken me.'

'Now look here, Rigsby. I will not hear of your staying at the White Hart. You must positively come to my house and stay a fortnight. Under that time I will not let you off; stay over it as long as you like.'

'Thank you. I do not mind if I accept. If anything has to be done to my dear Dulcina's jaw, it would be more satisfactory to be in your Rectory than in an inn. One cannot secure all the comforts requisite for an invalid at an hotel.

Should the tooth be extracted or the nerve destroyed, my daughter will be so shattered that further travel will be impossible for some days. The people at the White Hart are good and kind ; still an inn is not a place for a person with a carious tooth. Dulcina is made uncomfortable by the scream of the engines. Glastonbury is a terminus, and every engine that comes in shrieks to announce its arrival, and every one that leaves shrieks to proclaim its departure. Dulcina's nerves are in that quivering state of irritation that the least noise upsets her.'

'She shall come here at once. I will send my carriage.'

'We will come in the afternoon. I must go and see the dentist myself. I shall be able to judge by his looks whether he is intelligent— as for his experience, of that I cannot form an opinion. Has he studied in America? The Yankees are far ahead of us in dentistry. They transplant teeth as we do trees.'

'Wait a moment,' said the Archdeacon ; 'I will fetch Lady Elizabeth.'

He ran out of the room, and found his wife still engaged over the club accounts.

'My dear Edward,' said she. 'I will meet your wishes half-way ; I can do no more.

Betty Perkins shall have two-and-twopence instead of four-and-fourpence in each club.'

'Elizabeth,' exclaimed the Archdeacon, 'come into the drawing-room and see Rigsby. But stay—first give me the telegraph forms; I must send off at once for Saltcombe.'

'Why so? What has occurred?'

'My dear Elizabeth, Rigsby has an only daughter, worth ten thousand a year. That represents about two hundred and fifty to three hundred thousand pounds. Oh, Elizabeth! if only some of the Kingsbridge estates might be cleared with this sum, how happy we should all be!'

END OF THE FIRST VOLUME.

PRINTED BY
SPOTTISWOODE AND CO., NEW-STREET SQUARE
LONDON

By WILKIE COLLINS.

NO NAME. AFTER DARK. ARMADALE.

⁎ *The above may also be had in Limp Cloth, price 2s. 6d. each.*

By the Author of 'JOHN HALIFAX, GENTLEMAN.'

ROMANTIC TALES. | DOMESTIC STORIES.

By HOLME LEE.

AGAINST WIND AND TIDE. | BASIL GODFREY'S CAPRICE.
SYLVAN HOLT'S DAUGHTER. | MAUDE TALBOT.
KATHIE BRANDE. | COUNTRY STORIES.
WARP AND WOOF. |
ANNIS WARLEIGH'S FORTUNES. | KATHERINE'S TRIAL.
THE WORTLEBANK DIARY. | MR. WYNYARD'S WARD.

THE BEAUTIFUL MISS BARRINGTON.

By Captain GRONOW.

RECOLLECTIONS AND ANECDOTES OF THE CAMP, THE COURT, AND THE CLUBS.
ANECDOTES OF CELEBRITIES OF LONDON AND PARIS. To which are added LAST RECOLLECTIONS OF THE CAMP, THE COURT, AND THE CLUBS.

Uniform with the above.

GRASP YOUR NETTLE. By E. Lynn Linton.
AGNES OF SORRENTO. By Mrs. H. B. Stowe.
TALES OF THE COLONIES; or, Adventures of an Emigrant. By C. Rowcroft.
LAVINIA. By the Author of ' Dr. Antonio ' and ' Lorenzo Benoni.'
THE MOORS AND THE FENS. By Mrs. J. H. Riddell.
HESTER KIRTON. By Katharine S. Macquoid.
BY THE SEA. By Katharine S. Macquoid.
THE HOTEL DU PETIT ST. JEAN.
VERA. By the Author of 'The Hôtel du Petit St. Jean.'
IN THAT STATE OF LIFE. By Hamilton Aïdé.
MORALS AND MYSTERIES. By Hamilton Aïdé.
MR. AND MRS. FAULCONBRIDGE. By Hamilton Aïdé.
SIX MONTHS HENCE. By the Author of 'Behind the Veil,' &c.
THE STORY OF THE PLÉBISCITE. By MM. Erckmann-Chatrian.
THE CONSCRIPT, and WATERLOO. By M M. Erckmann Chatrian In One volume.
GABRIEL DENVER. By Oliver Madox Brown.
TAKE CARE WHOM YOU TRUST. By Compton Reade.
PEARL AND EMERALD. By R. E. Francillon.
ISEULTE. By the Author of 'The Hôtel du Petit St. Jean.'
PENRUDDOCKE. By Hamilton Aïdé.
A GARDEN OF WOMEN. By Sarah Tytler.
BRIGADIER FREDERIC. By MM. Erckmann-Chatrian.
⁎MOLLY BAWN. By the Author of ' Phyllis,' &c.
MATRIMONY. By W. E. NORRIS.
⁎PHYLLIS. By the Author of ' Molly Bawn,' &c.
MADEMOISELLE DE MERSAC. By W. E. NORRIS.
⁎MRS. GEOFFREY. By the Author of ' Molly Bawn.'
BEN MILNER'S WOOING. By HOLME LEE.
⁎AIRY FAIRY LILIAN. By the Author of ' Molly Bawn.'
FOR PERCIVAL. By MARGARET VELEY.
⁎ROSSMOYNE. By the Author of ' Molly Bawn.'
MEHALAH. By the Author of ' John Herring.'
⁎DORIS. By the Author of ' Molly Bawn.'
JOHN HERRING. By the Author of ' Mehalah.'

⁎ These Volumes can also be had in Limp Cloth, fcp. 8vo. 2s. 6d. each.

London: SMITH, ELDER, & CO., 15 Waterloo Place.

www.ingramcontent.com/pod-product-compliance
Lightning Source LLC
Chambersburg PA
CBHW031030120726
47905CB00007B/2123